THE SNOWS

REVIATHAN
BOOK 3

N K JOYNSON

For all those who wake up each day to reach for their dreams.
To my mother and father who taught me to imagine big and
then believe I could make it happen.

1

The Translator

The air rippled, catching the corner of Alandra's eye as she sat quietly analysing her latest discovery. The garden smelt of hyacinth and cherry blossom. The leaves swayed gently in the wind behind her. Then once again a sort of shimmer, and ripples almost like small waves this time flicked through the air right in front of her. Alandra lifted her head from the comfort of her book, only to be faced by the image of a small, pale-haired girl. She looked to be in panic, searching left and right for something. As she moved, the image flickered like a transmission that wasn't receiving clearly. This stole all of Alandra's attention. Shouldn't she be the one to be panicking by this strange sight of what she could only imagine to be the spirit of a young girl?

The girl spun around suddenly and stared directly at Alandra, realising she was being watched. Her eyes wide with surprise. She straightened up and composed herself. As she did so, the image grew sharper and Alandra could see that she was perhaps six years old, a small girl with a very slight build and dressed in a long party dress.

"You can see me?" The girl asked hesitantly.

"It seems so," said Alandra trying to keep her composure.

"Oh," replied the girl "that's very strange. Most people can't."

Alandra hunched her shoulders. "I have no idea why?" She replied "but you look a little flustered. Is there a problem?" She continued matter of factly.

The girl paused. It was obvious that she was confused at the strangeness of the conversation that she now found herself engaged in. She looked once again to her left and right, then back towards Alandra frowning.

"Have you seen Elie?" She asked indignantly.

"Who is Elie?" Alandra asked.

"My dog," the image replied, "it feels like an eternity that I've been looking for him."

"It might well be exactly that," Alandra replied ironically. "Do you know when your birthday is?" She asked gently.

"Well yes of course," replied the little girl, "23rd June 1976."

Alandra nodded. "I see. I think it's best that you sit down for a moment," she suggested to the little girl who did as she was asked, sitting cross legged on the ground in front of her. She looked up at her waiting for her next instruction.

"That feels better doesn't it?" Alandra asked her.

"I guess so," the little girl replied, suddenly feeling relieved.

"Now, this is going to seem quite strange to you, but I believe you are stuck in a paradigm. That means, to be clear, that you are stuck between two dimensions because you cannot accept to lose your dog. It would be much better for your well-being if you continue your transition to the other side."

"What other side?" The girl responded quizzically.

"Well," replied Alandra gently, "whatever you were doing when you died, you're still very attached to your dog. I can see that your mind is flooded with images of him and you are in such a panic that you can't think about anything else. You're going round in circles and you seem to have been doing that for a long time how."

The girl looked startled and then started to cry. This made Alandra feel quite uncomfortable.

"Ok, we can fix this," she said reassuringly. "You know that you just have to let it go. Accept to move on and you might even find that Elie is already on the other side since, on average, dogs don't tend to live for 100 years. According to my calculations, he'd be well, 117 by now if he is the same age as you."

"I'm 117?" Asked the little girl.

"Well technically speaking, no, you're still six, but if your dog is, well, still alive then he'd be 117, which of course is very old, so he probably also died by now. In fact, a long time ago."

The girl looked shocked and confused.

"Let's just say that, if you were to transition peacefully to the other side, he's probably waiting for you there and that's why you can't find him here!" concluded Alandra.

The girl's face suddenly brightened and as it did so, her image began to fade. In a peaceful gust of wind she was gone and Alandra was once again sitting alone. She noticed the garden was buzzing with insects going about their business. She sat for a moment thinking about the strange encounter that she had just been faced with.

It wasn't the first time this had happened to her. There was that time, around two years ago, with the little boy who had been in an accident. He was still in shock. Then there was another girl around the same age as her who was determined to finish her painting before she transitioned to the other side. Alandra already knew from these previous encounters that she could communicate with spirits. After all she could communicate with pretty much any living thing, why not people that were dead too?

Alandra was a member of the Snow tribe. The Snows' communication capacities were impeccable. They looked after the huge network of communication hubs that allowed all of the Reviathan tribes to connect with and translate for one another across the multiple languages they used. Their abilities ranged from recognising symbols and interpreting the sense behind images, to the whole range of alphabets and even telepathy. They were the world's experts in decoding messages and translating them into meaning. There was always a pattern and the Snow tribespeople just loved to organise and find the logic in any schemas in front of them.

The hubs weren't quite connected yet, there was still much work to be done to make sure that everyone was capable of connecting with other people. Some of the ancient languages weren't so used anymore. Only the elders could understand them and unfortunately many of the first generation inhabitants of Reviathan were dying of old age. All this wisdom and knowledge which had traditionally been transferred through stories and music in these old languages would be lost. Alandra found many of these old texts fascinating. As if they were a sacred part of a lost world. It was a world that existed before Reviathan, the Ostrich era as some people called it, before the environmental cataclysm that she had never herself known. She could spend hours deciphering the meaning behind the characters and symbols of these old languages and she just loved to explain what she had found to others.

The Snows were always working hard to keep the system upgraded with the latest techniques. Every time they learnt something new, whether from the innovative Sparks tribe or from pieces of history that emerged, they would rethink the best way to share or use the new information. Spending hours fixing something or solving problems didn't phase them. In fact they enjoyed it, gaining satisfaction from a job well done. Their values of hard work and transparency came from their Inuit traditions. They'd had to manage to communicate in the most difficult, icy weather conditions so they learnt to fine-tune their skills, which of course just became even more sensitive during the environmental cataclysm period. Good communication was a necessity for survival.

She decided that she would continue her studies of the ancient Inuit text that her Grandfather had given to her. It had belonged to her Grandmother, Elanor, who had also been fascinated by the history and languages of the other Reviathan tribes. She would say that "the voice was the doorway to the soul." It is not just what we say but how we say it that is important. Precision was the key.

Alandra's grandmother had passed away three months prior to her birth. According to Inuit tradition, as the last person to die in the family, Alandra would take on a certain number of her characteristics. They believed that their spirits were linked and even recognised the ancestor's qualities in the child. They also believed that literally everything, living or not, had a spirit and that is why a certain number of them could also communicate with the spirit world. Some would hear voices in their minds, while others, like Alandra could actually see spirits too.

It was widely accepted that Alandra's grandmother was an amazing translator and historian. For much of her life she had been one of the curators of the international archives. The breadth of her cultural knowledge was amazing. She could talk for hours about historical events, recalling the minutest facts. She would always make linkages to other events where she thought there was a connection between the causes. Her Grandfather was far less interested in the events themselves than he was in his wife. He found her capacity to recount such complexities absolutely wonderful. He was the type of person who loved finding clarity in anything complex. He was more of a problem solver himself, but he had much admiration for Elanor's ability to see and explain all these connections and he loved to encourage Alandra to develop these abilities.

According to Alandra's family, she had inherited her grandmother's curiosity and attention to detail. Alandra was meticulous and hard-working and she generally didn't miss a trick. She had all the potential of a budding translator herself.

Alandra went inside and carefully lifted out a dusty old book from a voice-activated, glass panelled cabinet. She placed it gently on a light-activated tabletop in the centre of the room. The flaking pages crackled gently as she turned them over, scanning the multiple lines of hand-written symbols. They had been carefully crafted and then the whole book was bound with a chocolate-brown coloured leather to try to ensure that it lasted through the ages.

Her grandmother had skillfully illustrated many of the pages with scenes and amazingly detailed diagrams of objects that were relevant to her accounts of the Inuit culture. Although based on a rich mix of different cultures, the Snow tribe founded many of their values on the Inuit's need for efficient and precise communication in the middle of some of the thickest blizzards that the Arctic circle and Alaskan straights could throw at them. They understood the importance of preparing ahead for these difficult conditions, even the slightest mis-calculation could impact their provisions or the tasks that the community undertook to live through long, dark winters.

She scanned the pages one after the other as she had done on so many occasions, hoping to unravel a detail that she had overlooked. She had translated almost half of the book into the languages of the other tribes of Reviathan so that they would be able to read it and understand more of the Snow tribe's history. It had to be said that Alandra was a bit of a perfectionist so she wanted to be sure that every word, every meaning that she attributed to her Grandmother's words were true. She had no intention of finishing the translation quickly but rather wanted to make sure that it was done well.

As she neared the end, her attention was taken by one of the last pictures, the scene of a plantation where people were happily labouring in the rows of thick vegetation. The text described a renewal of "New Earth". Alandra knew this place as the part of Earth that had been devastated during the environmental cataclysm. How could it be so green and lush? She had understood that it was like a desert. She concentrated on every detail of the scene. She wanted to understand it all. The way that the plants were grouped together, how they supported one another, how they survived in the middle of all of that desolation. Her Grandmother described it all. The surrounding areas were arid and mountainous. It was a strange contrast to the flourishing plantation. Alandra had seen pictures of New Earth but had never been there. The Youngers (young tribespeople who had not yet transitioned through their rite of passage) were not encouraged to go there because of the obvious dangers from the environment. There were few resources left and the chances of landslides were still very high. The plantation looked like an oasis in the middle of all of the nothingness of its surrounding environment. How can all of this ecosystem function so efficiently in the middle of that? Alandra questioned in her mind. It wasn't logical. They must have some state of the art technology to hand, or perhaps it was just the knowledge of the Seasons tribespeople that allowed everything to blossom.

They were amazingly in tune with with the cycles of nature, knowing the ways of each plant and insect down to the finest detail. They just loved to spend many an hour alone with their permaculture, studying the interactions between all of the parts of the eco-system and simply enjoying the quiet. They must have nourished all of that land with so much good intention for it to flourish like that.

The text spoke of how the Seasons tribe had made it their life's mission to revive the Earth once more. Then, turning to the next page, she saw how the plantation would be attacked. Curiously, it didn't say by whom or when. It wasn't like her Grandmother to leave out details but then it was at the end of the book which she had written during the final year of her life. Perhaps she hadn't had time to check all of the facts?

Alandra leaned over the book and squinted closely at the final lines. They were blurred and much smaller than the rest of the print.

Her mother, Nala, came into the room startling Alandra.

"There you are Alandra," she said as she launched into a detailed explanation without even taking a breath. "The radars are disfunctioning again, the coordinates seemed to be ok but they shifted a split-second to the right and they are now off trajectory. I need to go to the central bureau to see what's causing the distortion. I think it will only take about 34 minutes but I wanted to make sure that you and your brother are organised before I leave. Do you need anything from me before I go?"

Alandra took a breath. "No it's fine mother," she replied calmly "I"m just going to study this for a while." She replied, indicating the book.

"Your little brother is in the media centre, can you please keep an eye on him?" She added before leaving the room.

"Sure," Alandra replied somewhat lethargically. "What's he doing?" She called after her mother suspiciously.

"I think he was fixing your MessagePad," her mother called back to her as the door swooshed shut between them.

Alandra felt a cold shudder rush over her and panic take hold. "What?" She called out, but there was no-one there to hear her.

She rushed into the media centre where her brother, Sionis, was indeed lying on the floor rapidly keying code into her MessagePad.

"What are you doing?" Alandra shouted frantically.

Her brother looked up at her in surprise and abruptly stopped what he was doing. With a half-smile he held out her MessagePad. "I fixed the translator," he said proudly. "It was bugging when Mum used it this morning so I offered to look at it."

Alandra swiped it out of his hands. "Don't touch my things, not ever! You couldn't fix a document with an automatic spellcheck!" she added sarcastically.

Their father overhearing the noise, came into the room. "What's all the fuss?" He asked calmly, looking at Alandra, then at Sionis, then back at Alandra as he waited for one of them to give him an explanation. Then seeing that things were a bit too tense, and Alandra's concern as she held onto her MessagePad, he tried to reassure her.

"I can take a look at that," he offered holding out his hand to her.

He lit up the screen to reveal the translator module and quickly began to scan over the dictionary of each language at a speed that astounded Alandra.

"Arabic, check; English, check; French, check; Spanish, check; Norwegian, check, Mandarin, check, Hindi, check….." His analysis took less than one minute for each of them. "Seems ok to me," he concluded as Sionis beamed sarcastically at his sister.

"Hmm, just as well," Alandra replied "there would have been big trouble if you'd messed with anything!"

Sionis mimicked her huffiness, being careful not to be seen by their father.

"*Virus!*" She called out at him as she swung around and left the room in a huff.

Alandra liked to always know where her things were, to be organized. That way she had everything she needed to hand, all the information and tools she might need to do her best. It got her so frustrated when people moved things, and her brother knew very well that it pushed her buttons. They didn't get on so well together. He was always bugging her and she thought he was probably jealous of her being top of her grades, a 'know-it-all'. She felt sorry for him but it wasn't her fault and it didn't excuse his behaviour. He just needed to try harder she thought, after all she worked very hard to get things just right and she liked people to notice when she did. It made her feel special, like all the hard work was worthwhile. And then there was just this special gift that she had, she just seemed to know things : to know the right question to ask and just what someone else was thinking, telepathy.

She went back to her translations, taking a moment to carefully tidy her MessagePad into her bag so it didn't go astray again. She sat down and gazed at the open page. Funny that she hadn't noticed before. The symbols and words spoke of how life was on Earth before the cataclysms. It spoke of the difficulties that humans had to understand one another, even when they spoke the same language. It made her think about Sionis. She tried so hard to understand things and yet she had to admit that she didn't really get why her brother was just so downright awkward. Maybe they weren't any better now than humans had been before?

2

The Armenian scriptures

The room was quiet once again. Alandra's mother had left the house, and her father and brother had gone back to whatever it was that they were working on. Peace at last! Alandra liked nothing more than to be able to plunge for hours into her books. The big old book was dusty. She blew away a layer as she turned once again to the last page and then to the inside of the back cover. Concentrating hard on the final lines, she could make out a reference. It showed a multitude of symbols

enclosing a date at the bottom of the page which read "1st September 1974 when it all began." It was more than a century older than her. A shiver ran down Alandra's spine as she thought of all the generations that had come and gone since then, including her own grandmother. Then she suddenly felt that thinking about them brought her closer to them. After all their spirits were still around her, she of all people knew that.

She took a deep breath and composed herself to put the commotion with Sionis behind her. As she settled down once again to scan the symbols that surrounded the date, they almost seemed to jump out of the page at her, one by one. She deciphered tringles and spheres interlocked. They danced as if playing with her. She saw them shuffle around and bounce off one another playfully. Were they seriously trying to confuse her? Was she seeing things? Her mind was rapidly rearranging them in different ways to try to find some sense in them, some logic in their ordering or use. X (13) Aluminium...then T (31) Gallium...then M (20) Calcium... her mind raced. She let herself relax as her eyes flicked from one to another. Minutes passed. The sounds of each symbol rang in her mind as each appeared in her mind's eye. Why would there be three T's and then another M (93+20=113 or 31313120?), it didn't make sense. The T represented the Earth and M a man. Then she grasped it, they were ancient Armenian symbols. The alphabet had been rewritten.

Why would her Grandmother use these versions of the T's and M's that had not been understood for centuries, well before 1974? Alandra frowned as she thought hard.

Then she realised that they were alchemists, there was a code in the use of the elements. The symbols were trying to help her to find it. Their inter-locking forms revealed the location of a building where the book had apparently been written. The coordinates were 55°64'N, 122°34'W.

Alandra rushed to the interactive panel on the far side of the room. It blinked on. She quickly spoke the coordinates and a holographic representation of the location appeared. One small area showed the satellite view, whilst another displayed a zoom of what could be seen there. It was a small refuge.

Its frosted windows sparkled in the sun, reflecting streams of reds, yellows and greens across the surrounding grounds and foliage. A tiny gem in the middle of nowhere. She walked around the hologram of the refuge taking in all of it's aspects. It seemed timeless, a place to hide from life's difficulties, as if locked in its own peaceful capsule.

"If it's visible on the satellite system then it must still be standing," Alandra thought to herself. "How curious."

She felt a calling from deep inside her to go there. Her grandmother's quotes, as she had left them inscribed in various parts of the book, pointed to the absolute importance of protecting whatever had been preserved within the refuge walls.

"Don't be absurd," she heard herself say. "No-one goes to New Earth. The likelihood of a seismic shift is still in the range of a 75% probability. There is almost no clean water, the ground is arid and there is little to eat. The devastation has left a rancid, toxic sludge in many regions, covering the ground sufficiently to prevent life in any form from resurfacing. If anything happens to my supplies, I could starve to death. That's a 30% probability."

She started to run through all the possibilities and reasons why it was madness to go there. She felt a cold flush of anxiety. Something told her, however, that it was the only way that she would understand whatever her grandmother was trying to protect. There were more codes to understand, her grandmother's life work had to be completed. That was a task that she couldn't refuse. She liked the thought that her grandmother would have been able to count on her to finish the job and would be proud of her. This calmed her worries and gave her a sense of motivation.

What would she need? She started to think through all of the possibilities again but this time with a view to anticipating the different problems so that she could organise herself to address them as they came along. She came up with an absolutely huge list of supplies, 936 items!

"Impossible that all of that will go into my backpack," she sighed."No really this is madness."

By the time she had narrowed it down to twenty or so crucial resources she was feeling a bit more confident that she would be able to handle at least 50% of the possible outcomes. The rest she would just have to hope her usual resourcefulness would find the right solution over there. When all is said and done, she still had her MessagePad and her Regster so she could communicate and she was mobile.

Alandra convinced herself once again that it was the right thing to do. She would need to write a note for her parents, explaining at least where she would be and what she would be doing. If she was clear in her arguments and let them know her exact coordinates, perhaps they would be ok with her going there overnight, just enough time to find the refuge, see what was there and return. After all, she was only following on with her Grandmother's work. Once again she started to think about the strange symbols. "Why write in code?" She turned over and over in her mind. Normally Snow's liked things to be clear. Complexity didn't scare them, but creating it on purpose? Very strange.

She shook her head and plunged back into her preparation.

"Let me see, 300 kilometres at an average speed of 35 km per hour on my Regster makes 8 hours and 34 minutes to get there. Obviously the same to return," She calculated.

She gathered her supplies together and took a moment to test each part of her Regster. It had recently been checked by an expert so she felt pretty confident it would be fine, but she did a double check again just incase. Snows were known for their thoroughness.

Alandra entered a note for her parents into the communication system. Of course, it perfectly eloquently explained what she was doing, her whereabouts and her coordinates. She activated the geolocation on her MessagePad so that she could be traced, testing it against her current position to make sure it was clearly displayed on the interactive panel. Sure enough she was soon on her way out of her research room and the front door of the house.

Looking down at her device, she reviewed the coordinates of the refuge one last time and programmed her Regster to navigate in that direction on autopilot. She leapt onto the platform and only moments later she was heading towards the Reviathan border. A place that she had never adventured beyond.

3

The Narwhals

The frontier of Reviathan disappeared slowly into the background as Alandra advanced over the booming ocean waves way below her. Reviathan was an environment of lush vegetation that had been preserved from all the environmental destruction of the cataclysm because of the ocean that separated its island inhabitants from the mainland.

She had heard stories of the devastation from books and documentaries that she had studied over the years but she had never seen the mainland of New Earth with her own eyes. There it was, rising out of the horizon in front of her. It looked silent and hostile as the wind whipped along its coastline.

The MessagePad counted down the distance she was covering. "Making good progress," she thought to herself, feeling proud but at the same time apprehensive of what she might encounter there.

She drew her cloak around her as the temperature began to drop quite significantly. The wind had an icy edge to it, especially at the speed that she was travelling. Being organised, Alandra had prepared for these possibilities and slowed her Regster to a halt for a moment to reach into her backpack. As she pulled out a warm bonnet and placed it over her red flowing locks, her view of the shoreline came into focus. To her surprise, it was covered entirely with ice and snow.

She must have been only 8 or 9 kilometres away from the shoreline at this stage. It looked ragged and desolate. Her heart sank at the emptiness of the land before her. In an eerie fashion it seemed to be calling her name. She decided to progress cautiously. She could find her bearings once she arrived at her destination. Now wasn't the moment to become disheartened or turn back she thought to herself.

Alandra made her way along the fjords, still following the MessagePad directions, further and further upstream along the coast to what would have been the country of Canada before the environmental cataclysm. She saw the ice banks moving slightly, drifting below her. The geographic lines had changed significantly since the period of the disasters. Much of the North had frozen over as the streams of cold water shifted Southwards, and the Arctic had shrunk to be almost inexistant. The sea levels had risen greatly, engulfing hundreds of kilometres of once useful agricultural ground. Between the floods and the subsequent icy conditions that set

24

in, the old maps were no longer useful.

As she neared an enormous icy verge, Alandra tried to use her geolocation once again to double-check her position but her MessagePad just returned a long, hollow beep. "No that's not part of the plan," she thought to herself, feeling highly frustrated. She had no idea where she was and looked out over the horizon to find her bearings. In the distance there was movement on the surface of the ocean. An elegant flowing motion that kept breaking against the white peaks of the waves.

Closer to the ice bank, three narwhals surfaced. Two males and one female. They took her by surprise. Their enormous unicorn-like tooth protruded majestically from the water. They seemed at once both proud and serene. They bobbed gracefully in the passing waves as they held her gaze. They could sense that she was there. A narwhal's tooth is highly sensitive and can pick up the presence of food particules, changes in pressure and changes in temperature. They had noticed her arrival from a great distance.

She could sense their curiosity, but also their natural fear of her. Narwhals have been hunted for centuries by many tribes of humans to the extent that they were on the 'almost endangered species' list. That is, until the devastation. Perhaps there were more of them now? Now that they were left alone. She could see hundreds of them moving upstream in unison. An amazing sight which filled her with inspiration. Not everything is dead here she thought to herself. Their long migrations continue to give birth to another generation of Narwhals.

The male's backs were stained with black and brown

markings, the females were a greyish-blue. They began to circle playfully in the waters below her as if to attract her attention.

"At least you know where you're going!" She thought to herself. Their instincts were strong to return to their birth places. Alandra wasn't so sure of her own instincts at this moment. She pulled her cloak tightly around her. She thought about how her ancestors had hunted these graceful creatures. Part of her was happy that they were now free to migrate without fear that they would be attacked. Then, as she thought for a moment about their navigation paths, she realised where she must be. She remembered reading in the history books about how they would follow the same routes every year, tracked by her ancestors. If the narwhals go past Ridden Point, then across the Hevenar Straights, then we must be several kilometres upstream, parallel to the peaks of the Effring Heights. She could see the peaks of the mountains to the right of her. If she followed their base Southwards then she would soon be at the same gradient as Reviathan. She had been travelling in the wrong direction! The autopilot on her MessagePad must have been malfunctioning. She should have noticed! How could she not have noticed? She again felt herself fill up with frustration and then she sighed deeply as she noticed that she was being hard on herself again. She stood for a moment in calm to still her thoughts. Then it came to her. Once again she saw the image of her brother Sionis 'fixing' her MessagePad.

"Could he? Would he? Did he break something? Or even tamper with it to get back at her?" She thought.

"That little virus!" She blurted out as she stood there fuming, but there was no-one listening. Her words echoed through the bleak valley and back to her on the gusts of wind. It suddenly felt pointless to be annoyed, he wasn't there and it wasn't helping her to get where she needed to be.

She looked back at the narwhals who were still playing in the water below her. Perhaps they too wanted her attention? As she watched, her heart warmed again just a little. Part of her wanted to play with them too and forget about being frustrated.

"Thank you my friends," she spoke gently to them. "I don't feel so lost or so alone now because of you."

She looked around her and the crisp, cold wind whipped through her hair. She pulled her cloak tightly around her and set off in the direction of the South, towards where she hoped the refuge would be. It would be impossible to use her Regster in this freezing cold as it would most probably malfunction too and maybe even cause an accident. Alandra had calculated each probable outcome of using it and the probability wasn't very high that it would work out to her advantage. She often took the time to think things through, ask the right questions and then follow her logic through. So, she was going to walk, it was less risky. She didn't even know how far she'd need to go and yet she felt comforted by knowing that she was at least heading in the right direction now.

Putting one foot in front of the other, metre after metre, she progressed along a trailhead at the foot of the mountains. The tall flags of stone protected her somewhat from the wind and she sang to herself to stay positive. Hours passed. She must have walked for at least 20 kilometres she thought to herself. So she decided to stop for a while. The atmosphere around her had been warming up as she walked and there were now pockets of greenery sprouting through the ice and snow here and there.

She found a patch of grass which was in direct sunlight and settled herself for a moment. She was still feeling a little disheartened by her setback as she pulled out her MessagePad half-heartedly hoping somehow that it would click back into action. She swiped several commands on the screen, but nothing, it just kept blinking back at her.

"At least it's still alive," she sighed, trying to maintain a positive outlook. She gazed up at the sky, realising it was actually a beautiful day. The sky was turning a bright, crisp blue. In the corner of her eye, she noticed some movement. The usual signs of rippling energy that was becoming all too familiar to her and in the next moment, she was staring at an image of her grandmother. Her eyes looked compassionately at Alandra.

"History always repeats itself my dear," she said with a smile. "You'll find your way. You'll find what you need. Have faith, you are where you need to be. Find the book. It's important."

"But I'm in the middle of nowhere!" declared Alandra. "How can this be the right place for anything. That doesn't make sense."

"Does everything have to make sense?" Her grandmother asked. "Ok, that was a joke. I haven't forgotten I'm a Snow," she said with a giggle. "You're doing wonderfully, you've been very studious and I know you can do this. You're not lost, everything is relative, meaning you are closer than you think. This is the land of your ancestors. You're an Inuit remember. You LOVE the snow!"

"Relative to what?" Asked Alandra. "It would be much easier if you gave me the coordinates."

"I could, and that would be useful if you could put them into your MessagePad, but you can't," replied her grandmother. "Sometimes we have to truly believe in what we want and just set out in that direction, not just work hard for things without thinking about why. That means, for example, knowing why you're looking for the book in the first place."

"Because you told me to find it," Alandra replied.

"That's not enough," replied her grandmother gently. "You can't go through life just doing what people tell you to do. What do you want to find? It is important that there is meaning in what you do."

Alandra paused for a long moment, thinking through her motivation. "I think I want to understand our heritage, who I am and where I came from. Then after all it's my duty to share anything I find in the book with other people. Is that what the book will tell me?"

"What does your heart say to you?" Enquired her grandmother, encouraging her to go further.

"That there is a story that needs to be unravelled and to be understood, that I should be ready to question everything so I can make up my own mind about what is true." Alandra surprised herself with her response.

Her grandmother nodded wisely. "I'm so very proud of you

my dear. At the next fork in the pathway, take the left branch. Be safe little one."

Alandra sparkled in response to her grandmother's praise. She admired her grandmother very much so felt very touched by her words. Just as she was starting to feel better, with the next gust of wind her grandmother was gone.

"A very inconvenient time to disappear," she thought to herself as she picked herself up, brushed herself down and prepared to set off once again. "The path to the left," she repeated over and over in her mind.

Sure enough, several minutes later the pathway forked and as Alandra made her way along the stretch of dirt track that led Eastwards, she noticed the glow of an encampment fire in the distance. Her heart leapt with a mix of both joy and relief. She was greatly in need of some engineering skills to set her MessagePad right again but there probably weren't many Snows in the area.

As she approached she could see a group of horses tied to some nearby bushes. A fire was billowing smoke into the sky and there was discussion underway between three figures positioned closely around the fire. They were clearly nomadic Star tribesmen.

Alandra walked straight up to them feeling reassured that they would be willing to help. Stars are known for their mediation skills. They are seekers of truth and believe in not judging others so at least Alandra told herself that she wouldn't feel stupid announcing to them that she was lost. Perhaps they wouldn't be the best at fixing her MessagePad, since they're not exactly engineers like the Snows, but she was confident they would point her towards the nearest safe place to rest.

The eldest Star greeted her with a reverence that surprised and moved her. He had a certain calm, wise diplomacy about him that made her feel at ease. He was accompanied by two Star Youngers who looked to be around the ages of 17 and 20 years old. Each stood to greet her, touching their five fingers to hers to welcome her.

The youngest of them was wearing a long black tunic belted at the waist with a leaf green coloured sash. His features were fine and his almond-shaped eyes were a gentle, hazelnut brown. They looked warmly at Alandra.

"Hatham,' he introduced himself to her.

She could tell he was a Star because of the markings on his neck. They are all tattooed with a vertical line of three linked stars. They represent the positions of balance between the sky, man and the Earth. Stars make sure that their tattoo is visible to everyone so that they can be identified quickly as a neutral person in any conflict.

The Youngers continued to smile warmly but kept a certain formal, proud stance leaving their Grandfather to speak.

"My dearest Snow Younger, what brings you here to these parts of New Earth?" He asked her. Alandra could read in his thoughts that he already knew but she decided to reply politely.

"My MessagePad guided me in the wrong direction, it's malfunctioning," she added with a frown.

"I guess you're looking for the nearest plantation?" He continued.

"There are plantations near here? The ones that the Seasons are creating?" Alandra asked excitedly, remembering the pictures that she had seen in her Grandmother's book.

"Yes, of course," he replied reassuringly, "Belnite would be the nearest. It's only a few kilometres from here."

Alandra grinned spontaneously. She felt safe.

"Rest for a moment with us," the elder offered, "you seem tired."

Alandra thanked him and settled herself by the fire, taking a cup of warm hibiscus tea that Hatham handed to her.

The elder cleared his throat gently with a sort of hoarse cough. "You know young lady, Lao Tsu would say 'Trying to understand is like straining through muddy water. Have the patience to wait! Be still and allow the mud to settle' it is much simpler to find you way then." His soft brown eyes looked directly at Alandra but it felt as if he was looking through her. Like he was having a conversation with different part of her. It was very weird she thought. "He seems to be talking directly to my consciousness. To some sort of executive mind function that is as wise as he is."

She suddenly felt a little uncomfortable with Stars as they didn't show much thought activity. And when they brought back information from other dimensions of space and time it was like being side-bombed. Their reasoning just appeared out of know where. She had a hard time following their logic. Sometimes she wondered if it was even just their opinion rather than facts.

The elder sensed her discomfort with the silence and spoke after a moment. "I want to tell you a story," he said. The old man once again cleared his throat and began to tell her the story of Sai Weng.

"Sai Weng lived on the border and he raised horses for a living. One day, he lost one of his prized horses. After hearing of the misfortune, his neighbour felt sorry for him and came to comfort him. But Sai Weng simply asked, "How could we know it is not a good thing for me?" After a while, the lost horse returned with another beautiful horse. The neighbour came over again and congratulated Sai Weng on his good fortune. But Say Weng simply asked "How could we know if it is not a bad thing for me?" One day, his son went out for a ride with the new horse. He was violently thrown from the horse and broke his leg. The neighbours once again expressed their condolences to Sai Weng, but Said Weng simply said, "How could we know it is not a good thing for me?" One year later, the Emperor's army arrived at the village to recruit all able-bodied men to fight in the war. Because of his injury, Say Weng's son could not go off to war, and was spared from certain death."

He paused once again and looked at his guest, his eyes sparkled slightly like a dusty old gem. He gently concluded, "Life is not always what it seems. Look beyond the obvious. There is always a hidden gift."

Alandra nodded respectfully. She liked stories, especially when they had meaning. Although she felt welcome and safe, there was a strange feeling of 'deja vu' as she sat listening to the old man. She could read in their thoughts that they were still scanning her consciousness and for once this made her feel uncomfortable. She realised what it must feel like for other people when they knew she could read their thoughts. It was certainly just because of their curiosity. She knew that they could also see into the subconscious part of her brain where she didn't even know what she was thinking herself. The automatic part where all your actions are based on your fears or beliefs about life. Beliefs are important to the Star tribespeople. They had developed a gift for accessing this information so they could understand what motivated people to act as they do. It helps them with resolving arguments. She started to shift awkwardly in her seat and sipped her hibiscus tea rather quickly to keep herself occupied. The fire crackled in the silence that seemed to last forever. Hatham and his brother all the while smiled kindly at her but remained outside of the conversation, leaving the conversation for their grandfather. She wrapped her cloak around her once again, more to protect herself from feeling awkward than for the cold at this stage.

"You can simply head South from here," said the elder changing the subject. "As you arrive at a river crossing you can follow it for 200 metres and you will see the entrance to Belnite. They will help you with whatever you need."

Alandra thanked her hosts for their kind hospitality and guidance. She quickly determined that it would now be possible to use her Regster without too much risk so she unfolded it from her pack and was shortly on her way.

Only twenty minutes later she started to hear the rush of a river in the distance and as she approached, she paused at it's edge. Looking out across the horizon she noticed the movement of two people on the far bank. They were filling flasks with water. She analysed their movements and thought to herself how risky it probably was to drink water from there. It could be filled with any kind of toxicity.

One of them caught sight of her and called out but she couldn't hear what they were saying. She instead just kept watching.

"Alandra," she announced proudly.

"Draydon," he replied, "and this is Rethia."

Alandra analysed her two new acquaintances. They were clearly Seasons tribespeople but they seemed too young to be coming from the mines. As she sifted through their thought patterns which seemed very confused and perhaps, even intimidated by her she realised that they were lost. They weren't however, lost in the same way she was, they didn't seem to even know what they were looking for, their place. Interesting Alandra thought, how do you plan for that? She giggled. She decided to shift into 'helpful' mode and give them some feedback. It was clearly a little too honest for them to take in all at once but it was to be the start of an amazing friendship.

She didn't find tardyferons that she told them she was looking for, and it took a while to understand each other (in fact a tardyferon might have been easier to understand at times!). She realised later, however, that she had met two incredibly gifted and dedicated Youngers who were also looking for how they could contribute to improving the future of humanity. Like all of the Seasons, their mission was that the Earth would once again thrive. Despite their differences, this common wish united them. They didn't realise that at the beginning of course, not when Alandra met them, sort of in the same way that she hadn't any idea what she was getting caught up in either. It led them into conflict with a group of New Earthers that she hadn't even known existed. Boy was she learning a lot!

Several days later, Alandra found herself lying there looking up at the stars and thinking back to her first encounter with the New Earthers. Everything had happened so fast that it felt like a whirlwind and it was only now, in the quiet of evening sky that she was starting to take it all in.

Another familiar shimmer of energy appeared to her right and she slowly began to see the image of a young boy, probably 10 years old. He had big, wide, brown eyes, a slight build and was only wearing very simple clothes. His feet were bare and Alandra could tell that he was a New Earther. He didn't look at all flustered like some of the spirits she met. In fact he looked straight at her calmly as if waiting for her to acknowledge that she'd seen him.

"Hi," Alandra said to him. "You don't seem lost like some of the others."

"I'm not," said the boy, "these are my homelands."

"I see," replied Alandra, "so you're still quite attached to them?"

"I guess you could say that," he replied shrugging his shoulders. "A lot has changed around here though. People are getting really old!"

He scratched his head and as his head tipped awkwardly to one side, his ear fell off. With amazing reflexes, he caught it before it hit the floor and popped it back on, looking quite embarrassed.

Alandra's surprise was obvious and didn't help the boy to feel any less self conscious.

"You had an accident?" She asked gently.

"Yes, I was exploring and fell out of a tree. I'd never seen one before, they're really great," he said matter of factly, "it only hurt for a split second," He added as he shrugged his shoulders. "That's life!" He continued as he found the courage to laugh at his own situation.

"Yes, sort of, I guess," replied Alandra trying to determine if the boy was really joking or if he actually realised that he was dead.

"Anyway, I was just in the area and I wanted to say thank you to you on behalf of the New Earther ancestors. They're very grateful, you know. Well, for all you're doing here." He spoke in such a mature way that Alandra was quite surprised. "More than you think," he said. "The book, don't forget about the book," he reminded her.

"Thank you," she managed. "You're very welcome, but I haven't forgotten. If I commit to doing something, I always do it," said Alandra indignantly.

"Don't get distracted," he added. "There is a lot to do." He warned her as he started to fade.

"Wait," Alandra called after him. "Do you know what is in the book?"

"The future of our people," he called back to her as the final ripples of his energy disappeared into the night sky.

It seemed to her that the mission to find the book was taking a bit of a detour but her skills were needed at the Belnite plantation where she'd be translating for a while and she knew her Grandmother would have done the same. As a feeling of satisfaction filled her, she let herself drift off to sleep basking in a sense of calm. Tomorrow was a big day. She had agreed to guide a party of New Earthers to the nearby plantation where they would work side by side with the Seasons tribespeople to grow new plants and creatures to be reintroduced back into the Earth's atmosphere. They would need her skills so that everything ran smoothly. As always, she was happy to lend a hand to get things done. After all, she was a Snow.

4

New Earth Plantation

"Welcome to the Belnite plantation," Alandra announced loudly and proudly to the procession of New Earthers who were filing into the plantation behind her. She seemed to be taking pride in her new role as their interpreter. It made her feel very useful and she could sense that she was going to get lots of opportunities to explain how things worked around there.

She beemed as she led them into the main grounds, her red hair blowing wildly in the wind of the sandstorm that was starting to whip up around them.

"Lets go inside quickly," she called to them, "follow me!" She indicated the entrance down into the passageways that she now knew so well. As usual, faithful to her work, there was Jessriah, Kekoa's granddaughter, waiting for them.

After having a tour of the facilities and being made to feel at home, the New Earther's were starting to relax slightly instead of constantly being on alert. They asked many questions and some of them even started to take small roles in caring for the different plants in the enclosure.

One evening, several days later, one of the New Earthers began to talk about how things could have been very different for them if they had been aware much sooner of the existence of all of this technology. There were a number of elders seated in a circle and also quite a few Seasons tribespeople sitting around the edges of the room. They were listening into their exchanges from a distance.

The elders were comparing all of the methods of permaculture that they had been taught and the benefits of using Zana the central monitoring system's capabilities. They were impressed by what had been achieved at the plantation despite the harsh difficulties of the surrounding environment. A number of them were thinking about how some of the cultivation principles could also be applied back at their village.

One of the Seasons tribespeople, intrigued and enthused by their interest in the details of the methods, asked what kind of food they grew back at the village. This took the conversation to another place where the elders started to remember many of the hardships back home. They had been living with very basic supplies for many years now. They explained how they would plant and harvest, the whole village together. These were moment of celebration. They had an organisation where almost everyone tended to the land and contributed to ensuring that the community could continue to eat.

As she was busily taking notes of the conversation, Alandra suddenly caught sight of a young man watching her. He seemed to be intrigued by her fascination of their story and her avid attempts to record every small detail that was shared. He looked away, but she had already been quite distracted and realised she'd missed that last few sentences that the elder was sharing. "That could have been the most important part!" She found herself thinking. With that, she felt herself fill up with a sense of frustration that she forced herself to shrug off so she could throw herself back into concentrating hard. But every so often she noticed once again from the corner of her eye that he was staring at her. She started to shift uncomfortably in her seat. Alandra liked to analyse things but she didn't like being the subject of other people's analysis.

The young man started to turn over and over a stick that he was holding in his hands as if to distract himself, nonchalantly showing only a half-interest in what was being discussed.

"How do you get your water supplies?" another of the Seasons asked.

The room fell silent and the New Earthers looked at one another awkwardly. One of them then broke the ice in the room by telling them that the nearest lake was over 20 kilometres away but that they were worried that it contained more and more toxicity. Something didn't sound right to Alandra about that response. She could tell they were hiding something, but because she had been distracted, she had missed the opportunity to read everyone's thoughts. The subject had changed. She told herself that she would find another opportunity.

The story turned to the different moments where the New Earthers had had to fight for survival. Many families had fled from the first environmental disasters by moving to more stable and fertile ground. They left their comfortable lifestyles and learnt to survive in these more remote areas using much of their own ingenuity and what nature had to offer them. They sensed the danger ahead as their survival instincts were strong. They grouped together as best they could in self-sustaining communities, helping each other out where they could. Years passed and they became more and more isolated. Word spread of similar communities that existed. Radios kept them connected together, sharing news from one community to another.

People were scared and so they were taking their lives into their own hands. Were they well equipped? No, but they felt like they had little choice. The bush fires continued to rage and the tsunamis became ever more frequent. The communities foraged and exchanged goods to fulfil their needs. Outside visitors brought in equipment and supplies, or community members made visits to local abandoned towns to recover tools and furniture that people had left behind. They repaired and gave a second life to many items that others just threw away. Initially despite the change in lifestyle these communities thrived. People lived simply and depended on one another for support. It was when the environmental conditions really started to degrade that their fight for survival began. The air and water became so polluted that they had to move on several occasions, starting over each time. Then the land became dry, the plethora of forest animals slowly died out and the weather became temperamental. That was back in the 2030s. Each subsequent generation had to evolve their survival instincts in order to just exist. The conditions just got worse and worse, but their intuition became stronger and their knowledge of the underground water systems and areas of natural protection allowed them to protect their families.

"We have always been cooperative people," said the elder who was recounting their story, "this is why we never understood why you would not help us. We received news of the establishment of Reviathan through the networks. We hoped for many years during the 2040s that you would come to rescue us but you did not. You were only interested in your own salvation, in creating some new utopia for yourselves, forgetting your fellow men and women in need." His voice became filled with an undertone of anger and blame.

The Seasons elder Kekoa had been waiting calmly in the background for the opportunity to speak. "We did not know of your existence," he said peacefully. "During the 2030s, search parties were sent to New Earth but the conditions were so difficult that many times they abandoned their efforts. We neither had the tools, nor the communication networks available to us to act effectively. We were as lost and desolate as you were at first. We were simply lucky enough to have found the rich, fertile lands of the islands which were not affected as deeply by the disasters. In this space our technologies and capacities grew and we were careful not to upset this balance."

The elder whispered something to a fellow New Earther that Alandra did not catch and then fell silent. Another elder picked up the story, recounting the different leaders who had kept them believing they could make it through. How they had discovered new sources of food supplies just as things were getting desperate. They had always managed to pull through.

By the end of the evening, each of the elders had painted a picture of a tribe of amazingly astute, adaptable, courageous people who had fought hard to survive over the past 70 years with very little resources. Despite the fact that the Seasons had discovered them scavenging old refuse sites, here was an extremely proud tribe who had held together despite all the odds against them. Looking back of all that she had written and at the faces around the room, Alandra felt a huge sense of compassion for all that they had endured. She, of course also felt very proud that she had noted everything down so that the other Reviathan tribes would be able to read all of their story too. She felt a tingle down her spine as she suddenly thought of her grandmother, the great historian. She knew that she would have been proud of her.

5

Getting to Know You

The next day, Alandra was explaining some of the technical characteristics of Zana's data driven monitoring system to a group of New Earthers when, from the corner of her eye, she noticed the young man from the previous evening. He was once again siting alone twiddling a contraption that she hadn't seen before.

Her audience were very intrigued by Zana, this highly unusual piece of technology, but not nearly as much as Alandra was intrigued by the presence of the young man. She couldn't stop herself from looking over in his direction every now and again. The New Earthers were asking lots of questions and started to notice her distraction. She felt the urge to ask just as many questions about his identity and what he was doing here. He must have been around 17 years old, but he wasn't part of the original party. Alandra had gotten to know all of their names and stories. No, he must have just arrived and already he looked almost bored. Indeed, while she was watching him, he started throwing small stones against a nearby rock face to pass the time.

Her conversation with the New Earthers quickly came to a close given that Alandra wasn't even really listening to the questions anymore. They lost interest and started to wander around to inspect other areas of their new territory. This left Alandra with just the opening she needed to confront this strange person.

She strode up to him in her usual confident manner, ready to fire a string of questions at him but as she opened her mouth, to her surprise, nothing came out. She was standing right in front of him. He couldn't have missed the sight of her turning scarlet with embarrassment! Her brain felt frozen for a moment. He looked up at her amused.

"I never thought I'd see that! You finally ran out of things to say?" He rebuffed and he threw another stone against the wall.

His reaction shook Alandra back to her senses. "If you'd spent as much time cultivating some politeness as you do throwing stones against the wall then you might be worth talking to!" She said with a huff and she turned to storm off.

"Only joking," the young man replied "don't take things so seriously. You know you're good at what you do, so it doesn't matter what other people think about it."

Alandra looked back at him, hesitating a moment as she analysed him to see if he was being sincere. Given she could read his thoughts, she could see that he was being genuine and that he was actually worried that she was going to leave now.

"Ok funny guy," she launched, "tell me what you're doing here? You don't seem at all interested in what's going on. You seem, frankly, well, bored…"

The young man shrugged his shoulders and then just said "I'm here with my elder grandfather, Mandrid, I need to keep an eye on him so that he doesn't have an accident. He's getting quite old now and he tends to fall down or even wander off sometimes."

"How old old is he?" Asked Alandra

"We're not totally sure, somewhere around 80 give or take a few years," Said the young man.

Alandra scanned his thoughts and indeed it was clear that he had no idea.

"Alandra," she announced as she raised her five fingers to greet him.

"Sketch," he replied, touching his five fingers to hers.

Alandra smiled a little awkwardly. "So will you be staying here permanently with your grandfather?"

"I hope not!" Replied Sketch. "I have plans."

"Oh?" enquired Alandra. She wasn't getting any clear thought processes from him that showed that to be true. She frowned slightly while she waited for a response. Alandra always had difficulty to not say what she thought, especially when she could tell that someone was hiding something.

"I guess you'll decide as things progress," she reassured.

"Whatever," Sketch replied again nonchalantly.

He didn't seem very motivated by much on the outside but because Alandra could read his thoughts, she could tell that he was just trying to play it cool to impress her. He of course had no idea that she could do that. She suddenly felt quite flattered. She could see he was thinking about how awkward it was to make small talk. Given how he'd teased her for not knowing what to say she felt a bit more reassured. Maybe he even liked her.

"Well," she continued awkwardly, "best get to work, I'm only here for another fifteen days. No time to lose. I'm writing up as much of your history as I can recover, and connecting it all into a sort of family tree for you. It needs clarifying and structuring. What I have so far goes way back to 1956," she added proudly.

She continued enthusiastically, not noticing whether Sketch was actually following what she was saying or not. "I have to make sure everyone understands Zana and then there is the planning of the rosters for looking after the different parts of the plantation. They need to be validated by everyone involved. Phew..." she sighed.

Sketch was looking wide eyed at her. She was making him

dizzy.

"All work and no play hey?" he replied.

"Oh yes! No time to lose, see you around," Alandra shrugged and in an instant she was making her way back to the main bunker leaving Sketch to wonder what had just hit him.

The following morning as Alandra was inspecting the roster for the day, she noticed Sketch was sitting in the same place. He seemed to have no intention to lend a hand and appeared to just be sizing up what was going on. It was almost as if he was studying everyone's movements, watching them go about their business. She decided to approach him again.

"Hey," she tried to say as lightly and uninterestedly as she could. "You seem to like this spot. I guess you can see the whole plantation from here?" she asked.

"Need to watch over my Grandfather," Sketch replied.

Alandra made a face like she didn't believe him, and tilting her head to one side, she waited for another response. She could see in his thoughts that he was looking for another explanation, having realised he'd been caught out.

"Let's just say I'm watching everyone's strategies," he corrected.

"You're watching the timing, what people choose to do, how they do it and with whom," Alandra replied in her usual matter of fact way.

"And..." replied Sketch. "Is that a crime? Are you going to

report me to Zana for that?" He laughed.

Alandra huffed. "No, it's just unusual that's all. Everyone else is busy."

"I'm busy," replied Sketch raising one eyebrow. "I'm watching the system, understanding the people in it. People do dumb stuff sometimes because they don't think first about what's most important. They just launch into it or do what someone else tells them to without thinking if it's right for them. I don't like to waste my time."

Alandra was reminded of what her Grandmother had said to her about knowing why you're doing something. She became curious. "So what's important to you?" she asked, despite the fact that she could already see what he was thinking about.

"I'm calculating how much food and resources this plantation can provide in order to support the rest of the villagers. At the moment, you seem to be using it to do really detailed research. If you switched the land space over there and over there to growing food then you could produce resources for at least 40 families," he said pointing to two areas to the front left and right of the plantation entrance.

Alandra suddenly felt quite touched by his reaction. He did care about what was going on. Finally someone who thought about impact and doing things right.

"I see," she said "so what do you suggest that we plant? There is some highly specialised research in those areas at the moment. Plants that will one day be transferred back to other parts of the Earth. Where do we put them?"

"Can we eat them?" Asked Sketch rather sarcastically.

"Well, no, not all of them," replied Alandra, "but not everything on Earth is there just for our benefit. We're not the only creatures. The Seasons are trying to recreate a whole ecosystem."

"Yes, and meanwhile people are almost starving," he replied abruptly.

Alandra fell silent. "What do you suggest? How many families do you need to provide for? I will see with Jessriah if we can reorganise without disrupting the tests. The Seasons will know if there is a way, but of course we can't go faster than the cycle of nature."

"Soybeans, they're nutritious and don't need much water. They grew them in the desert for many centuries," Suggested Sketch.

"Yes," said Alandra sorting through her memory banks, "that could work. Their growth cycle is only 45-65 days." She smiled at Sketch.

He looked proud of himself for having made a suggestion that might just work. As the next days passed on the plantation, the New Earthers and Seasons worked together to reallocate some of the lands to food production. They talked, prepared the land and planted side by side. Jessriah watched over in gratitude for the understanding that was beginning to blossom between the two tribes. It wasn't the only thing that began to blossom. Alandra and Sketch began to spend more time together, discussing and planning bigger projects, perhaps for the other Seasons plantations in the region.

Meanwhile, she continued her studies of the New Earther's history, noting all the important dates and facts. A picture was starting to emerge of how they had learnt to depend on themselves to survive. Alandra was beginning to understand why they could be paranoid and defensive sometimes. At moments she caught a glimpse of her Grandmother's presence close to her, and she felt comforted that she was doing the right thing being there to help for the time being, instead of searching for the book.

6

Star Magic

The first of the new food resource areas of the plantation were beginning to flourish. The Seasons had managed to install a protective, highly resistant film around the areas in order to avoid contact with the sandstorms and otherwise over-intensive sun rays. It was made from a recyclable material that the Sparks tribe had been innovating for almost a year now and they were delighted to be able to test it under such difficult conditions. The results were really quite satisfactory. Zana was hooked up to each of the areas where the grains had been sown and the data she was sharing was excellent. The land was in perfect condition and the plants were sprouting nicely.

Alandra was so busy with her enthusiasm of the initial results that she almost didn't notice that Sketch was there. She was busy calculating all the possibilities of the final harvest based on the probability of different temperature and of some crop losses. She was so caught up in her work that twice she didn't hear him say hello.

Sketch was clearly quite upset and suddenly launched into an attack. "You spend all your time filling your head with all these facts and figures that no-one cares about. What use is that? Just tell us that there will be food, that would be good enough! And all that history, what good is that now?"

"It's useful to understand our history so that we don't repeat the same mistakes," Alandra replied despite her shock as his reaction.

"But people just do whatever they want anyway," Sketch replied. "You're just hiding in your books. Knowing all that stuff makes you feel more important than other people."

"That's unkind. Why do you say that?" She said now feeling quite perplexed "It's interesting to try to understand how and why things work they way they do."

Sketch turned to walk away. Alandra could read in his thoughts that he felt frustrated and guilty. Frustrated by her intelligence and guilty for having been unkind to her. It didn't stop there though. "She's just an arrogant upstart who thinks she knows everything, I don't need her," he was telling himself.

"You are just the most insufferable person I've ever met!" She called after him, but he didn't even look back.

Alandra's eyes welled up as she watched him walk away. She felt like she had nothing left to say to him. Even if he hadn't actually said those words to her, she could see them as clear as day in his thoughts and she felt the pain of them like a swarm of stinging bees, even if she wasn't going to let it show.

She stood there for a moment feeling slightly desolate. What did she do to deserve that? It seemed to come out of nowhere. Maybe he was having a bad day. Perhaps there was something else that was bugging him. Alandra started to go through so many scenarios in her mind. Perhaps if yesterday she hadn't said this, or if she hadn't done that. Then she found herself thinking about all of the things that he had said to her on different occasions, making links between these different moments to try to find some logic. It felt like some huge network in her head that was getting so big that she could feel the pressure building up. The chain of events didn't make sense. His words didn't make sense. Her mind felt as unclear as one of those snow shakers trying to figure everything out. Her thought processes just weren't there and she felt lost. There was no logic coming to her.

She sat disheartened on a nearby rock not quite knowing what to do with herself.

At that moment, there was a great swirl of energy in the air and as a portal opened, a young man stepped out of it and in an instant was standing in front of her. Hatham smiled.

"There's no conflict here," said Alandra half-heartedly. "He just left. You're a little too late."

"Yes, I know that." Replied Hatham. "I'm actually here just to speak with you."

"Oh?" Alandra retorted, somewhat surprised and feeling like

she was being singled out. "Did I do something?" She continued. "I'm trying to understand what went wrong, but I just can't work it out."

"That's going to be very hard indeed,' comforted Hatham. "Sketch is in a state of confusion. On the one hand he has feelings for you, but on the other it scares him and he feels inferior to you because you're very intelligent and he thinks that he isn't. It's sort of like he feels the need to pull you down a peg or two on occasions so that he can feel better about himself. He's full of fear and needs to be in control of the relationship with you. New Earther's seem often to try to control the situations that they find themselves in. They fear the uncertainty of what would happen otherwise. Their survival instincts are very strong and so they react quite quickly and without thinking things through sometimes."

Alandra could see that Hatham had a clear perspective of the situation. His thoughts were calm and flowed without judgement. They were orderly and logical to her so she listened some more.

"I guess what I'm saying is that he likes you and doesn't know how to handle that," concluded Hatham. "Be careful, however, because it means that he is trying to manipulate the relationship to his advantage so he can feel ok. He's not in a place where he can understand the impact that it's having on you. The confusion. The harshness of his words. It might continue."

Hatham fell silent for a moment giving Alandra time to digest his words. She still felt quite phased but somehow his words were helping her to understand and this comforted her. She always found it difficult when she couldn't make sense of a situation.

"Hmmm, I still don't think I know what to do about it though…." She said feebly.

"Don't worry," said Hatham, "it will come to you in time. You'll find your answer."

There was another blank. Alandra looked around as if hoping that the solution was going to spring out of the sky at her. Nothing happened.

"How come you came to help me to understand all that?" Enquired Alandra changing the subject to avoid having to find an immediate solution. "How does a Star know when there is conflict around?"

"We can just feel it. There is a difference between a healthy debate and a lack of respect for the other person. We all close down sometimes. Conflicts create ripples in the Reviathan energy fields. We can see them and read into them to see what's happening. It's like they are tagged with information about the dates and times of the conflict. We can refer to them sort of like a log book. Our mission is to keep addressing these blips, one by one. You were on my path as I was looking for someone, a very beautiful Star called Helencia," he said with a wide smile. "Last time I saw her she was reading one of your brother's blips."

Alandra felt distinctly awkward. "So I guess you know about my brother and me then?"

"Uh-huh," replied Hatham still managing to sound impartial.

"I can see how frustrated you are by his behaviour. It has been like that for at least two years hasn't it?" He asked gently, trying to put himself in her shoes.

"He's not really a virus," Alandra said sheepishly as if anticipating the next step in their conversation.

Hatham just smiled again.

"He thinks that everyone loves you because you're clever and that no-one thinks he's as good as you." He added.

"I guess I knew that," replied Alandra.

She suddenly understood Sionis' need to be recognised too. Did she really take up all the space? Did it frustrate him enough to do such a thing as tamper with her MessagePad? That was really dangerous! As her anger subsided, she suddenly felt a sense of compassion for him. It was the first time that she felt that and it took her aback. All the moments that he had annoyed her flashed through her mind, one after the other. It occurred to her that Sionis didn't really hate her, he just didn't like the praise that she regularly got for her hard work and brilliant results. He felt unimportant. She saw him struggling for their parents' attention. It must seem to him like whatever he did it wasn't good enough. Everywhere he went people said to him "Ah you're Alandra's brother?" It was a heavy burden for him to carry. He wasn't Sionis, he was Alandra's little brother. Although she helped him sometimes with his studies, she saw herself criticising him when he couldn't find the answer or he didn't try hard enough. She felt a pang of guilt when she thought about it. She could have helped him to be a better version of himself. Help him to understand what she already knew. She could have supported him rather than falling into this constant conflict. She could have done a lot of things....

"But I suppose the past is the past," she said to herself as she understood better now the rivalry that had grown between them. In fact, she wished that she was with him now. She wished that she was home with all of her family. Why had she gone off like that in the first place? They would be missing her by now.

"Sionis also had the misfortune to be linked to an ancestor that noone really respected greatly, his eccentric great uncle Messim. So people see him as being a little strange. They can't always follow his logic as it was highly developed. You could say he was a misunderstood genius actually," concluded Hatham. "Sionis's thought patterns are similar. They are so fast to make links between thoughts that other Snows can't follow them so they find him confusing."

"I had no idea," said Alanadra surprised by this revelation. "I thought he'd just found some way of blocking me out. You know like a transmission scrambler. He kind of does this thing where he sends you here and there and then left and right and then just blanks out. Like there's nothing, it's gone...very strange." Alandra made some very confusing movements with her hands to emphasise her point.

Hatham looked at her rather blankly. "Actually no...I'm not sure I do quite understand...what exactly do you mean?"

"Never mind," Alandra replied "It's clearly not important."

She was feeling a bit awkward from all the discussions and sat frozen for a moment not quite knowing what else to say. A certain sadness filled her which she tried to push back down inside, reminding herself why she was here at the plantation in the first place. Then it came to her that Hatham, having travelled so much might have seen the refuge where the book was written.

"Have you seen an Armenian refuge on your travels by any chance? It looks like this," she asked stretching out her MessagePad to show a photo to Hatham, and also feeling relieved about having the possibility to change the subject of their conversation.

Hatham took the photo from her and pondered it carefully. "Yes I believe I have seen this place," he replied almost mysteriously. His eyes suddenly looked distant and Alandra could see that his thoughts were recounting his visit there.

In his memory, the door creaked loudly as he entered the refuge. Inside, the lighting was dim and there was a strong small of incense wafting through the air. His attention turned to the paintings in each of the small alcoves, the staircases, and the hanging candles as he walked towards the front.

There was an elderly woman standing there surrounded by two men dressed in religious clothes. Hatham had come there to mediate a conflict. The year was 2045. The men were complaining that the woman was hiding something or someone. The woman was trying desperately to cover up whatever it was.

As Hatham appeared in their proximity the discussion stopped abruptly. The men asked kindly but firmly who he was. It was rare for Star tribesmen to go back so far in time. They could after all change the course of history in mediating certain conflicts so they had to be careful to manage the consequences. But it also meant that their tribe emblems were not easily identifiable as mediators so they generally had more explaining to do and were not always well received.

Out of a side room a shadow moved into view. It was the silhouette of a young woman holding a baby. She was pale and clearly worried for her child that she held close to her for protection. She stood waiting for her audience to speak. Her posture showed her vulnerability. The elderly woman spoke on her behalf, telling the men that she needed to find safety from the floods that had ripped through the valley where she usually lived. The refuge was positioned high on one of the nearby mountain faces. The woman explained that she had climbed for hours to reach them in the hope of saving her child.

"But we have no food," announced one of the men "it's not that we don't want to help but there just isn't anything left. We handed so many supplies to other refugees."

"She has nowhere to go, it would be condemning her to death if we force her to leave," replied the elderly woman. "Show some compassion. I will give her my food," She offered.

Just as one of the men was showing signs of stubbornness, Hatham stepped in. He explained that there was little left undamaged within a 30 km radius and both her and the baby would certainly perish if she was to leave. The floods had not subsided.

"The woman is wise, and gifted. She is a hard worker and will help you to care for others who may arrive here needing your help. She knows much of the traditions of Inuit survival techniques. That is how she made it this far," He continued.

The men were surprised by Hatham's ability to know all of these things, yet they felt in their bones that what he was saying was the truth. They exchanged a few words together and then agreed she could stay for a few more days until they could find more food resources from somewhere.

Thanks to Hatham's explanations she was safe, at least for a while. This may well have changed the course of her life thought Alandra. She looked at the young women closely. She was of Inuit origin? Her face looked familiar and at that moment she realised, it was her grandmother. Hatham had saved her grandmother. She must have been carrying her father in her arms. Alandra stood in shock.

"What's wrong?" Asked Hatham coming out of his thoughts.

"That young woman was my grandmother!" She stated. "She finally stayed there for many months until my grandfather found her. While she was there she wrote a book of our history. Of how our culture survived the great floods to thrive again and evolve into the Snow Tribe. She's a historian. Or rather, she was..." She smiled at Hatham, not quite knowing what else to say as she stood in amazement. Shows of emotion weren't really her strength so after a short pause she settled on a very sincere 'thank you'.

Hatham nodded. "That's just what I do," he replied although he was clearly very proud of having been of service, especially to such a noble cause.

"As a matter of fact I was just reading through her book which we have at home. It's full of references to places much like that refuge in New Earth. Places which have a significance for our people and none of us have ever visited since Reviathan was established. Not to my knowledge anyway," Added Alandra coming back to the facts of the matter. "I'm curious as to what we can learn from them. I suppose I'd also like to see what I can find out about myself too."

Hatham nodded. He could sense that her consciousness was trying to expand, to understand more about life. "Perhaps I can help you?" He offered. "I can certainly tell you where the refuge is based. I have the inter-dimensional coordinates here somewhere." He said going into his thoughts of the refuge once again.

"It's based some 200 kilometres to the North West of Reviathan. In a small town by Lake Topaz near the border with what used to be the district of Nevada. Such a beautiful region," Hatham added.

"So from here at the plantation, that would make us only...." She only took a second to calculate. "Really?" She noted with surprise at the result she'd found, "14.6 kilometers away!"

"I believe it does," agreed Hatham.

"I could be there in only an hour or so on my Regster," she concluded joyfully.

No-one will miss me here if I go there for a few hours this afternoon. I could be back by nightfall she thought to herself. She thanked Hatham again warmly and rushed back inside to organise her detour. He in turn stepped back into a portal that opened at the foot of the hillside, continuing on with his search for Helencia. Alandra's heart felt full once again with the adventure that lay ahead. She had found her motivation and she resolved to put the disputes with Sketch and Sionis behind her. This was far more important.

7

The Prophecy

As the small refuge came into view, Alandra slowed her Regster to take in as many details as she could of the surroundings. It was perched, as her Grandmother had described, on the edge of a cliff although it was surrounded by more rocks than vegetation now. It was no longer hidden but visible for miles around, weathering the sandstorms of time here in desolate New Earth. She wondered if there would be anyone inside. There were no lights, just the sunset casting a golden orange glow over the domed rooftop.

She veered her Regster towards the old building, taking a moment to circle around it once to get the full picture. All was quiet. Landing carefully in front, she folded her Regster into her pack and took a deep breath. She was finally here. She was feeling nervous but at the same time proud at having found the place her Grandmother had described.

The heavy wooden door at the entrance was hanging half-heartedly from its rusty, old hinges. It had clearly battled against many a sandstorm. After calculating the probability of it falling if she moved it, Alandra decided to bend underneath it instead to go inside. The hall was dimly lit by the last rays of sunshine of the day but there was an eerie stillness to the place and all at once she felt uncomfortable. The wind had also forced its way inside, right to the back of the building where there were many broken chairs and artefacts lying strewn around. There were small piles of sand and rubble accumulated in front of them where their presence had blocked the passage of the sandstorms. The smell of the place was musty and Alandra found it difficult to breathe. She lifted her scarf to cover her mouth and nose and, reminding herself why she was there, she proceeded into the refuge navigating between the shadows of the pillars.

From her Grandmother's description, she could make out the alcoves and the paintings, the winding staircase and there it was, the door from which she had emerged holding Alandra's father all those years ago. She felt a shiver come over her. "What was in that room after all?" She asked herself. "I'm here so I might as well investigate," she told herself.

She entered the old room full of curiosity. The light broke through the far window bursting oranges and yellows over the thick grey dust that had been accumulating for some time. Cobwebs were hanging off the sides of overturned benches and cupboards that were half-opened. She scanned the space from ceiling to floor. The golden light helped her to feel a little more optimistic because she was starting to feel quite alone. She took another deep breath and concentrated on the finer details of each of the cupboards. Her Grandmother had spoken of a chest hidden somewhere in this room that contained the book. Perhaps it was inside one of the cupboards?

Excitedly she noticed a large old, wooden chest in the far corner of the room. There was a pile of chairs arranged around it as if to hide it from view. Alandra's heart beat faster as she moved towards it, shifting them and old branches that were in her path. The thick layer of dust lifted into small clouds, making her cough and sneeze before it dispersed into the air around her. Her stomach turned summersaults on itself as she stood in front of the box, nervously. She took another deep breath and slowly lifted the lid which creaked heavily. As she did, there was a swirl of whitish-grey air that wafted up and away from the chest as if to escape, leaving a space for her to peer inside. She rummaged around, moving a few old candles and candlesticks to one side and, realising that there was nothing inside she felt a huge pang of disappointment. Just as she was standing there puzzled, however, she heard someone clear their throat behind her.

"It's been a bit cramped in there waiting for you. You certainly took your time!"

Alandra spun around quite startled to see the spirit of a nun standing behind her. She appeared to be the elderly woman that Alandra had seen in Hatham's memories of the refuge, only quite a bit older and frankly quite worn by the passage of time.

"I knew you'd look in the box," she said to Alandra, evidently feeling quite proud of herself for correctly predicting the outcome.

"That's where my Grandmother *said* that the book was kept," replied Alandra sarcastically.

"I had to move it for safe keeping," replied the nun, "and because of that I've had to stay here ever since to watch over it and of course to tell you where I put it!" She huffed.

"Makes sense," said Alandra, "But you probably don't need to complain about it since you *chose* to move it. So you're not really *stuck* here as such?"

"No, indeed, my dear," replied the nun "I can leave when I like. I know the way to the other side. We just have a little work to do before then," She added with a wide, disjointed smile.

Alandra drew back in disgust. The nun had almost no teeth and those that were left were black and rotten. Her wide grin made Alandra feel uneasy. She even noticed half a worm hanging from behind one of them.

"Oooh I see," she winced feeling quite glad that she wouldn't be able to smell any of the rot given the nun's spirit form. "Let's get to it then" Alandra added with a hint of impatience, "where exactly is the book?"

"In safe keeping," replied the nun evasively. "I just need you to reply to three questions so that I can be sure that your intentions are positive."

Alandra looked surprised. Her Grandmother hadn't mentioned anything about questions and she hated it when things weren't transparent. Surprises made her feel uneasy, especially when she wasn't prepared for them! She frowned but the nun had already launched into her inquisition.

"What brings you to search for the Book of Prophecies? Do you know what it is about?" Asked the nun, all at once adopting a very authoritarian tone of voice which destabilised Alandra.

Alandra concentrated for a moment. She had no idea. The point was to find the Book so she would discover what it was all about. Her Grandmother hadn't left much explanation really, only that it was important. She remembered her Grandmother's words once again, to know why she was looking for the book and she started to blame herself for not having taken the time to think about it properly. Then an idea came to her. Alandra looked directly at the nun, concentrating hard as she delved into her thoughts. She navigated along the imprint of her brain synapses, between the electro-magnetic pulses of her thoughts, identifying those which were concerned whatever the nun knew about the book. There was a particularly bright but distinct pulse where the nun must have brought the answer to mind. It was surrounded by an emotion of excitement. Alandra zoomed in on it and clarity came to her like an illumination.

"It's about the potential futures of New Earth and Reviathan, their battle for survival," she replied calmly.

The nun, looked rather surprised by the fact that Alandra had spoken the exact words that she had been thinking.

"Did you do something weird just then?" She asked suspiciously, curling her upper lip and frowning.

Alandra looked away from the nun, and just shrugged her shoulders. "Nothing *weird*. Was I right or not?" She asked looking back at her challengingly.

"Yes, you are right," the nun replied with still a hint of suspicion. "You read my thoughts didn't you?"

"You didn't say that I couldn't," replied Alandra nonchalantly. "In fact you didn't mention any rules."

"I didn't?" Replied the nun pausing for a moment, "no I didn't did I? How thoughtless of me," she continued, coughing to clear her throat and cover her embarrassment. "Right, well, rule number 1, you're not allowed to read my thoughts."

Alandra nodded in agreement.

The nun was now fussing somewhat. Alandra could see that she was gathering her thoughts. It all looked pretty cloudy in her mind. "Ah-ah," said the nun "You're looking again."

"Sorry, it's a bad habit I have, hard to stop," replied Alandra blushing.

The nun continued.

"Question two, what does this symbol represent?" She asked, whipping out an image of an inverted triangle with a tree inside it, that she swooped over to place right under Alandra's nose.

Alandra gazed at the image. She'd seen one like it before but she couldn't remember when. She anchored herself and prepared to run a scan through her own memory banks. Like files in a highly sophisticated system, at lightening speed she accessed, analysed and re-classed millions of images one after the other by sifting through the depths of her brain's hippocampus where all her memories were kept. She sorted with amazing dexterity, until her eyes brightened and she was suddenly filled with enthusiasm. There it was, just as she'd seen it on her Grandmother's desk painted in watercolours, the tree, the triangle.

"It's the symbol of renewal!" Alandra replied excitedly.

"Right," the nun acknowledged, smiling once again. "Your Grandmother talked about this symbol a lot. She was fascinated by its powerful simplicity, but you must be careful, because some things are not always what they seem. We must understand the motivations behind all people's actions to ensure there is sincerity."

Alandra looked quizzically at the nun, who at that moment launched forward and began to circle haphazardly around her. Alandra was startled and was suddenly quite frustrated by the spirit's unpredictability now that she had promised not to read her thoughts.

"So, what is your intention in seeking the book?" She continued her inquisition, "Why should I give it to you? What makes you so special?" Round and round she circled, making Alandra feel quite dizzy. The question shocked her and made her feel awkward. She knew that she was good at many things but yes, why give it to her? Why not someone else? And what if she got the answer wrong? She suddenly felt very nervous with the pressure she was placing on herself. She wished that her Grandmother was there with her now, and just as she was starting to feel like the burden was too heavy for her to carry, she saw the shimmering movement of spirits appearing one by one. Five, six, seven, eight of them. Proud, wise Inuit elders including her Grandmother. She didn't recognise the others. They each took a place in a tightly connected semi-circle behind her and opposite the nun. There was silence once again as Alandra witnessed the amazing gathering. The room was filled with a silver light which emanated from the group.

"Because you can see and communicate what others cannot, what others dare not. You work to find solutions where others would lose hope," said one of the elders whispering to Alandra telepathically.

She was taken aback by the elder's response and stood there slightly phased for a moment questioning whether she'd heard correctly or if it was just her imagination. She repeated the words to herself. I do appear to be able to see spirits that I know others can't see. That's true enough. And I guess that I work hard. Actually I like working hard and doing a good job of things. As she went through these ideas in her mind, she started to feel quite touched. As she realised that she was respected by the elders who were gathered around her, she noticed her self-confidence grow. Her body straightened and she felt quite alert and open. She felt herself fill up with pride but still there was an underlying sense of uneasiness.

"Wow," she thought "I can't say that."

She turned the words over and over in her mind, wondering if there was a different way to say them without seeming arrogant, but resigned herself to the fact that she might change the meaning if she did. She straightened herself, coughed awkwardly to clear her throat and spoke them to the nun in a low tone of voice.

"Because I can see and communicate what others cannot, what others dare not. I work to find solutions where others would lose hope." She paused waiting for a reaction from the nun. "You didn't say that I couldn't ask a friend...." Alandra added smiling sheepishly.

The nun had by this time, stopped spiralling around and simply looked down on her compassionately. She started to nod her head slowly.

"You sure remind me of your Grandmother," she concluded with another disturbing smile.

8

The Book of All Ages

The nun sailed off out of the room with Alandra following on quickly behind her. Beyond the broken chairs and tables there was an almost imperceptible door which the nun passed straight through. Alandra almost walked straight into it she was so busy trying to keep up. She pulled hard on the ornate, metal handle and swung it open to reveal yet another dark, musty smelling room. This time there was no light and Alandra could only just make out the form of certain objects that were placed against the walls. She reached into her backpack to pull out a nano-torch which, as it flicked on, lit the entire space with amazing intensity. She placed it on a table in the centre of the room.

The nun was floating patiently in the back corner of the room waiting for her. Below her, another chest the size of a large old suitcase was standing proudly on four legs. The nun indicated to her to open the lid. Alandra peered inside. It was lined with purple velvet. Nothing else. Alandra's heart sank once more. The nun giggled again and did a somersault.

"Sorry, couldn't help myself, the suspense was *killing* me," she laughed at her own irony.

"You're already dead," Alandra reminded her sarcastically. She huffed and looked crossly at her as if to say can we get on with it?

"Now, now, no need to get personal," the nun barked. "You can pull out the drawer that's hidden underneath," she admitted, realising with excitement that all of this time she had been waiting for this exact moment. She watched Alandra intently as she gently pulled it open. There it was, the Book of Prophecies staring back at her.

Alandra wanted to take in every detail of the cover, the writing, the symbols, the embossed covering that was still beautifully intact.

As Alandra flicked through the pages one by one, the nun started to recount the story. She had, after all, read it so many times that she knew the text by heart.

The pictures were painted by hand in watercolours. Each of them with very precise details of the scenes they depicted.

She saw scenes of the establishment of Reviathan. It showed Devon with Hafeez, his close friend and mentor who was of Persian origin. They were shown in the middle of one of their inspiring debates.

In the next picture there was Devon seated with the original founders, the researchers, the anthropologues, the biologists, the scientists, the sociologists all working together to try to find a way towards a new utopia.

The text talked of their differences, of their disagreements but that ultimately they wanted to find a solution together so through many nights and days of discussing, listening and reasoning, a picture emerged, then a framework of what they were trying to achieve. How could they take into account everyone's preferences? They decided it was possible as long as none of these preferences hurt another human being or restrained their freedom to make their own choices once a person had gone through their rite of passage.

As the months turned into years and the research continued, specialised groups formed with the intention of looking more deeply into how we could live in harmony with nature once again. Methods of cultivating food, ways of looking after our health, of producing energy, of organising our living spaces and of building communities. Each group volunteered to investigate the subjects that were the most important to them. This is how each tribe of Reviathan came to life and eventually contributed to society in ways that respected what they valued most.

One group believed in the importance of creativity, freedom and spontaneity. Another, the importance of living with, and learning from nature. A third group chose to follow the principles of transparency, clarity and organisation. A fourth chose continuous improvement, challenge and construction. Another believed that the most important was to live in community, love and ensure no-one was excluded, then finally the sixth group chose peace, harmony and dialogue.

As these tribes formed their distinct identities, their gifts also developed. In the pictures, Alandra could see each of them becoming more powerful as they lived according to their most precious beliefs. With the environmental cataclysm forcing them to find new ways of surviving and their growing understanding of life and nature, each person mutated to become what could only be described as an 'enhanced human being'. They let go of the ideas that they had about what was possible or not. The book depicted symbols and quotations describing this advanced state of humans and how it all came about.

The Sparks learnt to compose and decompose matter, to innovate more effectively. The Seasons learnt to mimic, feel and live in harmony with nature. The Snows, to communicate in highly advanced ways, including through telepathy. The Streams learnt to harness and channel natural energy sources. The Sunsets could heal simply by being in their energy fields, and the Stars used their amazing ability to time jump in order to be in the right place and time to resolve conflicts.

They decided to use their gifts to contribute to a new kind of society, Reviathan. The Sparks would use their creativity to innovate, the Seasons would manage food and resource production, the Snows the communication systems, the Streams would ensure the use of clean and efficient energy supplies, the Sunsets would manage the social network and the Stars would mediate differences of opinion which might otherwise have led to continued disputes. All the tribespeople worked together to make sure that they had a role and could contribute fully to making things work for everyone.

Alandra scanned the pages where Reviathan became an established state. She watched as families migrated in droves to its safer, fertile lands, away from the natural catastrophes.

They were welcomed by those who were already there, setting up camps and infrastructure little by little. The children found new friends and the adults contributed to community projects. Each of them selected the tribes that they wanted to join. The tribes spent time together but there was no segregation, people were free to come and go between the areas where each tribe lived and worked.

Everything seemed peaceful as Alandra looked at the pictures, even if the early years of Reviathan were hard. People cooperated together for the benefit of all.

Her eyes were suddenly drawn to the next page. She saw the same scene she had only recently been a part of, the devastation of the Belnite plantation. There was Jessriah, Kekoa's granddaughter standing over the destruction. The book described in detail the sadness that the Seasons tribe had felt in discovering that their plantation had been ransacked.

Then on the next page she saw the meeting of the Reviathan tribes with the New Earthers. A chill ran down her spine. There in the front, standing exactly as it had occurred, she saw herself. She was interpreting for the New Earthers surrounded by the Seasons tribesmen. Yargen the Star tribesman was there, as were Kekoa, Drayden and Rethia. Each part of the scene was just as it had unfolded and the text spoke of the pact that had been made between the two sides in order to find peace and continue working to restore the Earth. Alandra was mesmerised. She stared at the page for a moment in disbelief. How was it possible? How could someone have known that this encounter, this very scene would occur? What if she hadn't even come to New Earth? None of it would have happened. It felt extremely strange to her. She reminded herself that the book had been written almost a hundred years ago. It was a prophecy and the strong realisation came over her once again that she was part of it all in some way.

She turned the page quickly to see what came next. She saw the New Earthers working in the plantation. Then, when she arrived towards the middle of the book there it was, right in the centre clear as day, the sign of Renewal. There was a picture of a man holding the tree and triangle symbol that she had seen on her Grandmother's desk. The one that the nun had spoken about. Why there, at this stage? What was his role in the story? She remembered the nun saying that the symbol was not all that it seemed. She stared for a long time at his face.

"So, that's Dorzak," interjected the nun nervously.

Alandra looked up startled. She had been gazing so deeply at the man's face that she had forgotten that the nun was even there.

"Who is he?" Alandra asked full of curiosity. "It says that he's a Stream tribesman who formed an opposing group." She paused. "What does he want with the New Earthers?" She asked pointing to a group of villagers who were standing to his left.

The nun looked gravely at Alandra. "I believe he's actually looking for excitement in any way he can find it," She replied. "The book says that he has different ambitions to the rest of the Stream tribe. He has been rallying all those Streams who believe in dominating other 'weaker' humans."

Alandra nodded. "I have met many Stream tribespeople," she said worriedly "I think most of them are interested in building quality, solid results, in using their power wisely and for everyone's benefit, not so much in breaking things."

"Unless it's to improve them?" The nun butted in raising her eyebrows to add another layer of wrinkles to her already heavily aged forehead. "He believes that it's ok to bend a few rules and break agreements in order to make progress and achieve the results everyone is looking for. It is said that he is willing to do almost anything to ensure that Reviathan becomes the great nation that he believes it was meant to be."

"Progess, yes, I see," added Alandra "I understand better. I guess it's a question of opinion as to what represents progress." She concluded, tutting to herself.

"He's a very powerful man," the nun confided, while also cautioning Alandra. "And he doesn't like to be crossed. He manipulates people for amusement. He sets them against one another and watches what happens. He finds it very funny and often the people don't even realise he started the whole conflict in the first place."

Alandra winced, "How awful! Why would someone do that?"

"As I said," the nun reminded her, "boredom can cause people to do all manner of unusual and destructive things. A lot of people actually believe that his intentions are good. You see?" She said pointing to the next page where there were Stream tribespeople and New Earthers listening to his speeches. "He is very charismatic and has quite a following already."

Alandra eagerly turned the next pages to see what happens, but as she scanned quickly over the text she understood that after the scene at the Belnite plantation, the prophecy spoke of three different possibilities that could occur. She followed each thread to understand the outcome. In the first, the group of Streams led by Dorzak would harness the Earth's energies to create a powerful nation with the New Earthers working for their benefit, while Dorzak's manipulation makes them think that the Stream tribespeople are helping and protecting them.

A second possibility talks of great battles between the two nations of Reviathan and New Earth. Each believing that they are defending the Earth. Alandra's heart felt heavy as she looked at the pictures of destruction and betrayal.

The final possibility showed peace between the tribes. It explained that Dorzak's power had been curbed but frustratingly for Alandra, there was no description of how. It spoke only of there being a weakness in his powers.

"Typical," huffed Alandra. "Why can't prophets be more explicit? They're quite happy to skim over important details as if the idea is enough. Too bad for those of us that actually have to do something about it. Oh no, they can't make life simple can they? Not their problem is it!"

Alandra was becoming quite stressed. She could feel nausea coming over her.

"I just need to sit down for a moment to think all of this through," she indicated to the nun. "I just need a moment. No, air, that's what I need air."

She was starting to fuss. "Need a plan. A bit of organisation. Everything will be better then," she was trying to reassure herself but her head was starting to spin.

A moment later the nun was floating above her, trying to waft some air onto her face. Alandra found herself lying on the floor looking up at the ceiling.

"You fainted," the nun said matter of factly.

"I did didn't I," replied Alandra feeling slightly embarrassed. As her eyes focused and she looked above her, however, she noticed a sphere painted there on the ceiling. It was an ornately black and gold globe which was surrounded by ancient inscriptions. She squinted to read it carefully "Դյուդ կանգնի՝ դերան կկոտրի"

"That's it!" Alandra yelled springing to her feet. "If the whole village stands, it can even break a trunk. I have to gather the tribes!" She thought to herself.

She ran outside and looked all around her, analysing the angles of the refuge compared to its surroundings and the direction of the sun. She swiped furiously to run a few calculations on her MessagePad and there it was, she realised she was right in the middle of a major rift. Exactly where the book predicted a landslide would occur.

She ran back inside to tell the nun what she had discovered but she was already gone. The book lay in the middle of the floor underneath the inscriptions, opened at the page where all of the possibilities started to diverge. In the picture, she saw herself once again, standing in the refuge, holding the book. A small red-haired girl, just as the prophecy had foretold. She took a deep breath to compose the overwhelming sense of responsibility she felt and looked up at the inscriptions once more. As Alandra stared at them she noticed some smaller inscriptions. She took out her MessagePad again and used it to zoom on each of the images in turn, capturing them so that she could refer to them if she needed to at a later time.

She sat cross-legged on the ground to study the text in more detail, but as she did so she felt some shaking. In the beginning it was like a tiny rumble, that became stronger and stronger until both she and the room were shaking. Tiny pieces of the ceiling began to crumble off and fall to the ground. She stood up, wrapped the book into her cloak and ran outside again.

The sky was a heavy grey and a storm was brewing overhead. The trees were starting to bend in the wind and rocks rolled left and right into the distance, pushed by the currents of air. She started to enter the coordinates into her MessagePad to calculate her distance from the eye of the storm. The numbers were flashing in front of her as they calculated, but a larger flash caught her eye. A portal opened in a circle of white energy and out stepped Hatham once again.

"I knew I'd find you here," he shouted over to her through the claps of thunder echoing in the background "quickly, no time to lose you need to leave here, it's not safe."

"I'm looking for the origin of the storm so I know what direction to go in," Alandra told him "you can't exactly take me with you through your portal," she added sarcastically.

"This is no ordinary storm. The origin, my dear Alandra, is coming from Dorzak's followers. They know you are here and they are on their way to recover the book now that the nun has gone. They also knew of its existence. They are Stream tribesmen who have invoked these elements to slow you down or even endanger your life and their powers are great. According to the prophecy you were the only one who could take the book from its resting place but now, the future can be influenced according to all of our choices. You must go now. I alerted the Seasons at the Belnite plantation nearby. They are on their way to help you. Go that way, zig zag down the back of the rock face on your Regster, it will protect you from the storm. You will find the Seasons tribespeople at the base of the mountain waiting for you."

The storm was growing stronger and clearly getting closer. The rain lashed down and lightening struck either side of her. As she disappeared over the edge of the cliff she saw the form of three men walking towards her, arms outstretched towards the sky. As one of them flicked their hand in a forward motion a blast of lightening struck just to the right of her where fortunately there was an old metal post sticking out of the ground that once served as a barrier.

Eyes wide with fear, Alandra, descended as far as she could while struggling to keep her balance in the strong winds. Her Regster hit the side of the cliff twice, throwing her into a spin so that she had to concentrate hard to regain control. Sure enough, there was a circle of Seasons waiting for her at the base of the cliff face. They closed inwards to protect her, covering over her with a tent-like structure. Their hardiness, having adapted to the harsh conditions of New Earth and its mines kept them all federated and unafraid of the storm.

They walked in unison with Alandra in the centre, protecting her from her perpetrators who watched the scene from the cliff above. They pushed forwards and onwards through the storm and towards the plantation. Flashes of lightening were reconducted from the protective covering above Alandra's head and into the Earth below. On multiple occasions there was a loud boom as it hit the surface, making her jump.

Rocks dashed onto the ground in front of them and the wind howled, yet the Seasons remained firm. In their hearts they also knew that Alandra was the only hope for regenerating New Earth back to its former glory. Their faith in nature kept them fixed on their mission to bring her back to the safety of Belnite. Onwards they strode, with speed and determination, walking for over an hour. It was the most secure option as the Streams kept up their offensive.

As they approached the Belnite plantation all of the Seasons, and some of the New Earthers, including Sketch rushed out to meet them. The wind still howled across the rows of plants, flinging some of them into the air, and lightening bolts struck in their path startling the welcome party.

"Fall back inside everyone!" Called Jessriah "We'll be safe in the tunnels."

"I think we're going to need all the help we can get," Alandra thought to herself as she realised that the battle had only just started and it was wasn't at all with the New Earthers where they they had assumed it was. The New Earther's paranoia was nothing compared to Dorzak's determination to succeed.

9

Zana

Alandra hurried into the safety of the underground tunnels of Belnite. Those same familiar smells and magenta lights helped her to relax again. She sat in one of the calmer corners of the main enclosure, not far from Zana, the plantation's faithful, and highly playful central monitor. Her job was to track the progress of all of the plants and creatures who were thriving at the plantation and suggest adjustments in how they were cared for based on their bio-feedback. Her internal systems were softly humming and tiny pin-points of lights were flashing intermittently across the screens showing the evident distress outside of what were usually thousands of happy plants. Alandra could see all in one go the extent of the Seasons' life work at Belnite. Millions of hours of analysis, understanding and nurturing had been channelled into this state of the art centre, designed to regenerate life and reintroduce it back into the desolation of New Earth. She couldn't understand what logic would cause someone to want to destroy all of that?

She watched the flashing lights settle one by one as outside, the Seasons scurried about trying to reinforce the protections. Yet, this was no ordinary sandstorm.

It was late in the evening and she was exhausted but time didn't seem to matter to her. She sat in quiet contemplation, trying to work out a strategy as to what she should do next. She replayed the scenes at the refuge in her mind and it all seemed surreal. Perhaps she was still in shock? Then she suddenly felt a huge weight of responsibility on her shoulders again. "Three possibilities," she reminded herself, only one of which really made sense to her. Just the thought of the other possibilities made her fill with defiance. She needed to understand more about this Dorzak person. Who was he and what did he really want?

She picked up her MessagePad and started to carry out a few searches to find out more about him. She heard a whirring sound and different images appeared in front of her, one after the other. Pictures of him speaking to different audiences, receiving awards, showing off his work. As Alandra stared at the images, they started to freeze on her screen, stuck in the same loop. She tapped furiously on the screen, trying to remove them but they weren't budging. Her MessagePad appeared to be malfunctioning once again.

"Oh rats," she yelled "not now! You can't do that to me! How am I supposed to get anything done around here?"

She felt a flurry of anger rush over her as she thought again of Sionis tampering with it, but since she actually had nowhere else to go and he wasn't there to argue with, she just sat there. As she sat with her anger she once again remembered her discussion with Hatham about her little brother needing recognition. She took a deep breath and as she did so, her anger turned into a feeling of understanding. She looked around the room feeling quite helpless and wondering what to do next.

In that moment of stillness, there it was, the inspiration came to her in a flash. She could ask Zana for help. The Snows were known for their highly developed communication systems. Alandra could upgrade Zana's system to monitor not just the plants but perhaps even Dorzak's movements. All she needed to do was to work out how to integrate some extra communication modules. She felt a rush of enthusiasm.

"Zana," she asked, standing in front of the computer's main sensor, "I need your help to track something else. Something very important. I'd need to add one or two more programs to your assets. Would that be ok for you?"

Zana stopped monitoring the plants for a moment and flashed a panel of lights in excitement. Although she was both reliable and highly precise, just like the Sparks there was nothing that she loved better than some spontaneity!

"First of all I'm going to need some technical help," Alandra thought. No other Snows around here and so I guess I need to contact home. First thing's first, "Zana, can you connect me with sector 15, enclosure number 6 please?" She asked politely.

Alandra's mother, Nala, flashed onto the monitor.

"Alandra!" She cried in relief, "we've been so worried about you! Where are you?"

"My monitor malfunctioned and, well, I'm in the Belnite plantation in New Earth"

"We got your note but we couldn't connect to your MessagePad. What could possibly have driven you to go to New Earth? Are you safe? Her mother gasped. By now she'd been joined by Alandra's father and her brother Sionis who was sheepishly trying to blend into the background of the room. He was curious to know where she was but feeling somewhat guilty that his practical joke had turned sour. He hadn't intended for her to fall into danger.

"I"m safe, surrounded by Seasons tribespeople. I really can't begin to tell you what has happened, it's almost surreal," replied Alandra feeling awkward. Sharing even the facts with her parents seemed quite strange. She wondered if they would believe her.

"Try us," her father encouraged. "I think we deserve an explanation."

Alandra spent the next twenty minutes recounting all that had happened to her in the minutest detail. She could see that her parents were shocked but they didn't intervene. They just let her explain. At the end as she fell silent, her father nodded slowly.

"Your Grandmother *was* quite unique," he reminisced. "I could tell that she was hiding something, but she was so committed, all her life she kept studying our history to understand what our future might be. What we could learn from it to become a better civilisation."

Alandra felt reassured that they understood. Despite all of the emotion she had managed to explain everything, honestly and clearly. That's important to a Snow tribesperson.

There was a silence as no-one quite knew what to say next. They were taking it all in.

Alandra cut in. "I have a plan!" She said excitedly. Suddenly thinking that the situation needed another dose of enthusiasm. "I was thinking that it would be a good idea to upgrade Zana so she can monitor what Dorzak is doing. We'll be able to see where he is causing disruption or holding his conferences to generate support for his cause. To start with though, we need to understand more about how he operates. The more we know about him, the better we'll be able to organise ourselves to act. Mum, I need your radar experience to add an extra protection to the plantation grounds. Dad, I need your help to add some new tracking components to Zana's core system, and Sionis, she paused... I need your knowledge of scrambling techniques so that we can intercept and divert their messages. What do you think?"

Sionis beamed. Alandra could see that he was feeling proud of being recognised for his abilities and especially that she wasn't mad at him. Her parents looked at each other. She could tell that they were going back over the details of what would be needed to put those kind of capabilities in place. Alandra could see their thoughts, the electro-magnetic pulses zapping around, as they organised their next steps.

Her father nodded. "Yes, I can transfer that to you through the Alpha Light Network if you think you can access it from there. The Seasons must upload their research there, probably through Zana so I imagine she's already connected."

Her mother added "and I can activate one of my extra radar devices from here and through the monitor I can transfer the view so that you can see the entire perimeter fence of the plantation, provided that it's no larger than 1.2 kilometres in surface area? That way I'll also know that you're safe until we get there."

Alandra was surprised. "You're coming here?"

"Of course my little bookworm, we wouldn't leave you there alone to deal with all of this would we? I'm sure you can, I mean, but I figure you might use our expertise there," Nala concluded, trying to show that she believed her daughter but her experience also told her that this would need to be a team effort.

Alandra was quietly happy that they were coming to be with her, but even more excited about her plans for Zana.

"Ok let's get to it then!" She cheered.

"I'll start to prepare the upload right away," said her father. "You'll need the enhanced identification application, a recognition device so we know which part of the system we're connecting to, and a Panther Tracker device linked into the mainframe."

"And I'll find the radar equipment and start to initialise that," added Nala her eyes twinkling at the idea of installing a new relay. "It will need quite a few tests."

Sionis was clearly thinking through all of the options to scramble the Streams' communication network. Alandra could see his mind racing now she understood a little better what he was doing and how his thoughts branched out laterally into a whole multitude of possibilities. She watched in awe at how rapidly the connections were made.

"Got it," he said as the frenetic calculation of options stopped and suddenly his thoughts went quiet. With that he hurried out of the room to prepare his part of the plan of action.

Alandra stayed online with her father as he guided her through the system upgrade.

"Ready Zana?" She asked the bubbly computer. Zana's lights flashed once more and a "Ready!" Appeared on her main screen. "Here we go then," Alandra announced as she proceeded to upload the first program, then the second, adding all the necessary components. Zana blinked new icons onto the monitor and rebooted to incorporate all the changes. After only half an hour there she was proudly displaying her new features.

Alandra was busy testing the access to different communication networks. She could see the buzzing of thousands of conversations here and there. All they would have to do is work out which channels they would need to track but it might take them a while. Let's start by bringing up some information on Dorzak to find out who he really is.

"Let's see, what do we have here?" she mused as she skimmed over many articles that described events in Dorzak's life. "It says he is an elder in the Stream community, very respected for the infrastructure that he's helped to build for the community. He was the team leader of the first group to put the kinetic fountains of water supplies in place and has a team of around fifty Streams who work on different energy projects with him. He's always trying to find new ways to improve the way we generate and use energy to make more power with less."

They stared at the different images of him, trying to understand his thoughts and motivations for causing such potential upheaval if the prophecy was right. Tall, dark, sharp blue eyes, broad shoulders and a very proud stance. He could clearly serve out heaps and heaps of charisma whenever he chose to.

"He looks like a politician to me," said her father sceptically. "Something unnerving about that smile of his. Enigmatic but fake. I bet he takes the credit for everyone else's work."

They were interrupted by her mother Nala. "Ok honey we're good to go. I've set up the relay and I can see your movements. We just need to set the coordinates of the perimeter of the plantation.

Alandra felt a burst of relief. Once that was set up they, and the book, would be safe. They would be able to see any movements of potential intruders outside. She rushed to the entrance to find Jessriah and get some help with the measurements. There she was, still watching the storm from afar. The three Streams who were responsible for the storms seemed to have set up camp on a cliffside overlooking the plantation and were watching the Seasons movements. A number of Seasons tribespeople had themselves set up a vigil around the plantation that they were intending to maintain throughout the night.

"I hope they're not planning to attack?" Worried Jessriah, "I don't understand what they want with us."

"They won't want to declare an outright conflict," Alandra replied. "That would be far to risky for Dorzak's reputation. No they'll try to be cleverer than that." She added, her mind already starting to strategise their different options.

Jessriah felt slightly reassured but was still searching for answers. "Who are they and what do they want? This plantation has had enough trouble. We are still clearing up the mess from the New Earther's ransacking. We could do without so much attention. Can't they just leave us alone to be in peace?"

Alandra smiled at her but in her usual matter of fact way she told her the truth of the situation. "So I doubt very much that they plan to leave us alone," she concluded, "but I do have a solution for you," she beamed. "I just need to know the coordinates of the plantation's perimeter?" She asked.

Jessriah thought for a moment. "It goes from the small baobab tree on the front left, to the cliff face to the right of the entrance, then behind the entrance to the tunnels, right back towards the river."

"Hmmmm...it's not very precise but I can work with that I guess. You never measured the place?"

Jessriah shrugged her shoulders. "We just keep planting where there is space," she replied.

"I see," said Alandra as she analysed the area that spread out in front of her. "Ok well, we'll set the entrance to the tunnels as the central point and then cover 65 metres North and

Southwards, and then 45 metres East and Westwards. That gives a surface area of 1.17 kilometres square. Best we can do for now," She sighed.

Jessriah looked confused.

"We installed a radar," Alandra beamed again. "You know, so we can see their movements. Come, I'll show you the rest," she beckoned towards the tunnels and Jessriah followed on behind her, full of curiosity.

"Tada!" Alandra yelled as she revealed the bright, enhanced version of Zana. Even her lights were now different colours.

"We needed colour coding," she added seeing Jessriah's surprise. "It's important so that you know which program is running or alerting you, otherwise you might think it's the plants invading," Alandra laughed at her own joke.

"Wow, that's amazing!" Jessriah enthused. She felt a huge surge of gratitude come over her as she felt that plantation would be safe now. They could continue their work, hopefully without intrusion.

Alandra felt very proud of herself and her family. She glanced back towards the monitor to see if they were still connected and had witnessed Jessriah's delight. Indeed her parents had and were beaming. Sionis at that moment, ran back into the room and raised his hands to show her a strange-looking object he was clutching. He too was looking very proud of himself.

"We just need to connect it into the main frame," he suggested. "Otherwise it's ready to go!"

"I guess we'd better make preparations to leave then," their mother suggested. "We'll be with you as soon as we can honey. Until then the radar is set on the coordinates you sent over. We'll test it again when I arrive. Take care. Think before you act!"

With that, the monitor blipped off and the two friends were left in the quiet of the main sector of the tunnels.

"Let's get to work.We have a plan to put in place!" Alandra encouraged.

Jessriah smiled. "Do you mind if I take a look at the book?" She asked curiously.

"Be my guest," replied Alandra. "I have some data to collect for now, but let me know if I can help with any explanations."

So she went about her business, checking over Zana's new functionalities and zooming into parts of the mainframe to gather information and set tracking applications.

"We'll soon find out where they are and what they're up to!" She concluded confidently.

Jessriah flipped through the pages until, just like Alandra, she came face to face with her own picture in the plantations ransack.

Alandra decided to leave her in her bubble for a while and continued to search. She carefully watched the monitor as she manoeuvred through the system, searching for Dorzak's whereabouts. Yesterday he was at a Sparks convention handing out awards for clean energy inventions. The day before he had been at a Seasons gathering where he was commending their Youngers for their recycling projects.

"Let me see, here it is," she spoke to herself out loud, "24th January, that's today but there's a blank and his geolocation appears to be switched off."

"Zana, can you connect to the satellite systems to look for any gathering of more than 10 people?" She enquired.

She scanned over the faces in the crowds as one by one Zana flashed up the pictures of all of the meetings taking place across Reviathan.

"He must be here somewhere," thought Alandra, starting to worry somewhat that today of all days, he wasn't traceable. "Well, he's not one of the Streams camped outside the plantation," she said as she struck that off her list of possibilities too. "But maybe he is in New Earth somewhere? Zana can you also scan gatherings in New Earth?" She requested.

Sure enough, his face could be seen in the middle of an immense gathering of New Earth villagers. Alandra froze as she stared at the screen. It was worse than she had imagined. The battle had already started without her and she watched their movements from a distance feeling quite powerless.

10

Dorzak The Captivator

The rally was literally spilling over with New Earthers. The elder chief had called a gathering of other inhabitants from many miles around their central encampment. They were swarming into the village square where a podium had been erected for Dorzak to be seen by everyone.

It was a sight to behold. Men, women and children all talking among themselves. They were wondering why they had been called together and who was this strange man who did not speak or dress like them. To the left of Dorzak stood a young man, a New Earther of slight build, but with a strong, glaring presence. He was Yorin, Dorzak's right-hand man who he had spent two years mentoring and teaching him Reviathan languages. He had planned this moment down to the finest detail, including his speech to the New Earthers to convince them of the importance of building an alliance with him. He would explain how the communities of Reviathan were their enemies, coming to steal their grounds and take the few resources that they had because of the population pressure in their own world.

As Dorzak arrived on the podium the crowd hushed. The chief was also by his side as a demonstration of support. It was clear that Dorzak was feeling confident and self-important. He took a moment to look over the crowd making eye contact with as many of them as he could. It was a way of gaining their trust. He had waited for this moment for a long time and was relishing the attention. He spoke firmly and confidently, every word translated by the faithful young man at his side.

"Welcome my friends. Thank you for gathering here today," he announced. "I am here to meet you in peace. To warn you of the terrible invasion that has started to take place on your sacred lands."

"You have worked hard to survive here. You know the secrets of this land. You are survivors! I can and will help you to continue to survive because I believe that this is wrong. The nation of Reviathan believe they are stronger and better than you. They think they can outwit you by offering you meagre peace agreements while continuing to take your resources. These are just small crumbs compared to the luxury they already have in Reviathan and yet they continue to take from you. I can help you to be more powerful, to meet your needs with energy that you cannot imagine today. My team of Streams are on their way here to support you. To help you to build an infrastructure that will protect and sustain you from this hostile post-cataclysm environment of New Earth. Everything here, without having to leave the place you call home. Your children will thrive!"

He paused and looked over the crowd once again for effect. Raising his arms towards them, he continued.

"A set of plans have been laid out," he indicated as two Streams rolled out a huge canvas with areas designated to be supplied with different energy types. Diagrams showed how the Streams would channel water from some hidden underground reserves into their villages.

"Your chief is a wise man. He sees the potential in this alliance. He has told us of the existence of an underground oasis of clean water. The project plans before you show how we will channel the underground water supplies to the surface in order to make the area fertile. We offer our gifts of being able to redirect some of that water to the surface, not only to nourish the land but so it will serve as an energy source to make your daily lives easier. You will no longer have to walk long distances each day to access this source. You are brave and you deserve to be rewarded for your efforts."

The crowd cheered in response. Then there were gasps of amazement as some Streams, who were standing over some strategically placed basins of water, demonstrated how they could channel the water in different directions using their bare hands. The New Earthers had never imagined that it was possible to move water in such a way. There were small children who ran around behind them to check that it wasn't trickery. They were expecting to see hidden levers or traps. There were none. Was it possible? Was it magic?

As the Streams' show skills came to an end, the New Earthers stood around discussing between themselves or moved to study the plans laid before them with much curiosity. Dorzak let them talk for a moment and then once he noticed that a number of them were nodding their heads, he broke the silence.

"Together we can make your land even stronger!" he called out proudly.

The crowd cheered once again, yelling and waving tools or staffs. The chief took Dorzak's arm and lifted it into the air triumphantly. They cheered even more loudly.

Dorzak stepped down from his podium and, led by the chief, he made his way through the excited crowd to where the other Streams were standing. Many of them patted him on the back or nodded at him to show their support for his ideas. This made Dorzak even more confident in his plan. He had successfully gained the alliance of hundreds of New Earthers. Things would be easier from now on.

The other Stream tribespeople were grinning widely in the knowledge that their plan was taking shape. Happy to have participated in the excitement of this historical moment. They knew that through the alliance, they too would have access to more resources than they could imagine.

Alandra had managed to witness the whole scene from safety of the Belnite plantation. She stood in shock as she realised the impact of such a pact. The chief had given his word to Kekoa, the Seasons elder, that there would be peace in return for handing over the Belnite plantation to the New Earthers. The chief was betraying that trust because he would gain even more through an alliance with Dorzak. She felt disgusted by the deceit and manipulation that Dorzak was coordinating in the shadows, out of sight from the

102

communities of Reviathan. It was now clear for her, Reviathan and especially Kekoa needed to know what Dorzak was up to.

What was also interesting was that she now knew that there were hidden pockets of resources that existed in New Earth. Given the desolation and toxicity present in the soil, clean water had become by far the most precious resource. This discovery would help the Seasons continue their work to regenerate the land and plant life here if only they could maintain the peace agreement with the New Earthers. They wouldn't just be able to go and help themselves to it, however, especially after the speech that Dorzak had just delivered to the New Earthers. How could they convince the New Earthers once again of their sincerity? That the water would be to nourish the Earth. To work together with the Seasons? How could they hope to compete with Dorzak's plan? Alandra pondered these questions deeply until she realised that she might be able to find some answers in the book.

She rushed over to Jessriah who was still holding it and started to flick through the pages. The three possibilities were starting to separate significantly, she could see it.

They saw Dorzak and his followers drawing water from the pure sources of New Earth. They were lifting it to the surface with their kinetic abilities. The New Earthers were waiting at the surface with containers to be filled. Many were cheering or even dancing. It was like a holiday for them. They could see that their lives would be much easier from now onwards. They could grow crops to eat and wash their children without having to walk for miles or use the toxic water from the rivers and lakes.

But the text talked of betrayal, of Dorzak diverting a part of the water for his own use. He would use it to reward his followers for their loyalty to his cause. He would convince the New Earthers to plant many crops which he also intended to take a proportion of. Instead of using their extra time and freedom for activities that they enjoyed, the villagers would instead organise themselves into groups who would create even more resources. Despite that fact that they felt happier and would be a little freer, the reality behind the scenes was that they were to become slaves to Dorzak's cause without even realising it. Alandra was shocked by the deceit that she was witnessing. The tribes of Reviathan would all be banished from New Earth, as if they were the enemy. Without the Seasons' continued work to nourish and regenerate the land, resources would once again just be used to survive without thought for the future generations. The book merely gave clues, however, and did not say how any of the three possibilities would end.

In the second of the possibilities, Dorzak would take over Reviathan through his political dealings. He would convince people of his wish to make Reviathan great. Through pitting tribespeople against one another and maintaining the New Earthers in conflict with them. He would position himself as a saviour of Reviathan, all the while manipulating both sides to stay in power. Alandra felt even more disgust as she turned the pages. Rebel factions would emerge on each side, trying to protect their own interests. They would each argue about what was most important because they lived by different values and they would put up barriers once more between the different sectors of Reviathan. Each tribe would live in fear of what they could lose rather than working together to create a society where everyone benefits. It all looked like a nightmare to Alandra. Again, there was no knowing where it would take them all.

Then there was the third possibility. She paused for a moment and took a deep breath, hoping that it might bring a better solution. Alandra saw a society of Reviathan and New Earthers working together to regenerate the Earth. The story spoke of harmony, of each side finding peace and thriving. As she flipped to the next page, she once again found herself standing aghast. There was a picture of her and Sketch standing side by side. The text spoke of the importance of their friendship. Despite her surprise she wanted to know more, but who should arrive in the sector at that very moment but Sketch himself. Much to Jessriah's surprise she hurredly closed the book firmly. It made a loud 'clack' and the noise resounded between the glass panels around her. She blushed the same magenta colour as the lights around her and just to cap it all, Zana's icons blinked excitedly as she giggled at Alandra's awkwardness.

"Shhhh…" Alandra snapped at her, feeling rather annoyed by Sketch's unexpected entrance.

"What are you doing?" he asked with his usual note of paranoia.

"Nothing," replied Alandra. Then she started to feel guilty for not being totally honest.

He could sense that she wasn't telling the whole truth and looked at her curiously.

"We need to inform Kekoa and the others about the book's contents and about what Dorzak is up to," she said in a worried way, also changing the subject.

Sketch nodded. "What exactly does it say?" He asked.

Alandra indicated to him to sit down and she took a moment to explain the three scenarios to him. Sketch asked lots of questions as they progressed. How? Why? When? Even though Alandra didn't have all of the answers, she felt reassured that Sketch was interested and committed to helping her. After all, the other New Earthers had just become Dorzak's followers. It was important that the ones who were already at the plantation believed that the Reviathan tribespeople were peaceful. They decided to rally the others to warn them.

"I know how to convince them," reassured Sketch. "In any case they are all asking questions about what's going on." He leant over and kissed her on the cheek. "Don't worry," he continued, "we can do this! There's always a solution."

With that he sprang to his feet and rushed back out of the tunnels to assemble everyone.

Alandra sat there for a moment, now feeling even redder than the magenta. Zana lit up a heart on her screen. "Don't you dare," replied Alandra. She started to tap wildly on Zana's control panel to remove her little joke but it wouldn't budge.

"Zana?" she pleaded, "it might be funny but it doesn't help much..."

The screen blinked off just as a crowd of New Earthers and Seasons tribespeople arrived.

The elders sat at the front, closing their eyes to listen intently. Kekoa, the elder of the Seasons tribe was there to support them. He had been waiting patiently in the compound for Alandra to be ready to share what she had learnt. He knew she would. She's a Snow tribesperson after all. Experts in communication, and some of the best analysers around. He knew she would make sense of what was going on.

As she came to the end of her explanation, one of the New Earther elders, Sketch's grandfather leaned forward to speak.

"It was a curse that you people came to our lands. We were safe until then. Now we are caught up in your factions, all looking after your own interests!"

Alandra could read in his thoughts that he was clearly angry and although he wasn't saying it, he felt guilty that his people had been misled and were starting to follow Dorzak so it was easier to blame the people of Reviathan. She was ready to speak again when Sketch intervened.

"Grandfather," Sketch replied, "we are caught up in this because we chose to believe Dorzak without thinking of the consequences. But also because we have a role to play in helping the Earth to thrive again. It is our home and you have seen the good work that these Seasons tribespeople are doing here. You have seen it with your own eyes. It is not just in our interest to support them, it is our destiny. Their future is now linked with ours. The book says so. If we turn against one another then Dorzak has already won. We have to have faith and work together, we don't have any other choice."

His grandfather looked directly at him for an instant, rehashing all of the information he had just received. He then nodded solemnly in approval.

"So, what's the plan?" Launched Alandra. She looked around at a room full of blank faces. "Hmmm...we could do with a few more Snows around here so we can get organised," she thought to herself, amused as she was starting to understand the tribes' different ways of looking at life.

She turned to Zana to show them the new monitoring system and how the radar worked. Then as she turned the monitoring system back towards the village they could see that the Streams, including Dorzak, were making their way towards the underground water sources. A party of eight people were heading North from the villagers' encampment. She could see the panic in the villagers eyes, and read in their thoughts that they were in disbelief that their chief was taking these strangers to such a secret and very sacred place. This was their lifeblood. Without these pure water resources, the villagers would perish.

The Seasons meanwhile were full of enthusiasm at the knowledge that these pockets of resources even existed. This meant that the Earth had reserves that she could draw on. The desolation was on the surface. How many of these existed? There could even be many of them. They started to think about how they could find them? It was a great idea to bring the water to the surface so long as there was sufficient amounts of the resource and they don't over-exploit it. It was a real sign of hope to them, just as Alandra had expected. Their faces were all radient and Jessriah's eyes were welled with tears. They were clearly not thinking about a plan at that moment in time but dreaming of new possibilities for the Earth to flourish again.

Sketch interjected once more "what if we just go back to the village and round up the Streams. There are only eight of them and they don't look so scary to me. We might be able to get them to confess what their real intentions are?"

The New Earthers looked at one another. There were only ten of them but they were surrounded by many more Seasons tribespeople.

"What if the other villagers don't believe us? What proof do we have?" Asked one of them out loud.

"They will never listen to us above the chief," added another disheartened.

"We have Alandra's recordings," Sketch added encouragingly.

"What if we can't trust these Seasons people? They will probably want to take the water resources for themselves once they know where it is!" Another New Earther spoke with veracity looking around the room at the others.

This shook the Seasons out of their dream state, remembering the importance of the problem in front of them. Dorzak was at this very moment causing havoc.

"I don't think we can just walk into the village and say 'Hey there, this man is a phoney,'" Alandra said matter of factly. "Anyone can create false news. We'll need to show them the book or catch the Streams red-handed, right in the act of stealing. Right now we have no firm proof and to be clear, all he has done so far is arrange for the water supplies to be brought to the surface to help the village. That's positive.

Only the book says that he will steal from them in the future." She paused.

"No, violence," she warned Sketch, "attacking head on won't help. It will just make us look bad, like we have no other means. We need to be cleverer than that." She concluded. Then she turned to face Zana. "What do you think Zana? Can we catch him?" She asked.

The monitor sparkled as her lights once again did a Mexican wave. "Of course!" Flicked across her screen. "All we have to do is monitor their whereabouts and then record parts of their conversations and scramble others to avoid the ressources being taken to wherever their hidden storage is. We can create a diversion!"

"Would it help if some of us go back to the village to stay among them? We can pick up intelligence or place transmitters locally. They won't recognise us so they won't know that we're checking on of their movements."

"The only ones who know we are here and aware of their scheming are the Streams who are keeping watch over the plantation here," one of the New Earthers added, "we'll have to avoid being seen when we slip past them."

"They're still pretty busy whipping up their storm outside to keep us occupied," another person spoke from the crowd.

Sure enough, as a small party of Seasons arrived at the surface, they saw the Streams stand up and ready themselves to call up the elements once again.

11

The New Earth Factions

Over in the New Earther's encampment, Dorzak had been busy discussing the infrastructure plans with a number of elder villagers. Some of them believed that the water should be brought to the central square of the village, others thought it should be close to the chief's home or their food storage. There was already a high level of disagreement between them and of course Dorzak saw an advantage in keeping them divided. He let them squabble between themselves and watched with delight.

"Let me know when you have decided," he called over to them. "I'll be waiting at the outpost."

His band of Streams were waiting for his instructions. The routes were in place to lift the water to the surface. From then onwards the villagers were free to do as they wished with it. What they didn't notice was the Streams making preparations to remove some of the resources. They had prepared alternative subterranean tunnels through which a certain proportion of the water would pass as it came up to the surface.

Alandra was watching from Zana's monitor. She started to panic as she saw what they were planning. The feeling of fear filled her whole body and she couldn't think straight. She tapped a few instructions but they didn't seem to integrate well with Zana's mainframe.

"What to do?" She asked herself over and over, but her thoughts weren't getting any clearer. The Streams were setting the coordinates for where the diverted resources would be sent. She could see them making their preparations. "I have to understand the patterns in their codes," she told herself.

Her father came into the area at that moment and seeing that she was in a panic he rushed over to her.

"What's wrong Alandra, you're almost hyperventilating?" He wrapped his arms around her and turned her away from the monitor for a moment to look him straight in the face. "Take a deep breath, you need to calm down and tell me what I can do to help you?" he held her steady for a moment whilst she came back to a state of calm.

"Father, they're stealing the resources, the book said that he would betray the New Earthers and look, on the monitor, they're doing it, right now. They're preparing to steal their precious water resources and I don't know what to do. I can't seem to program Zana to zoom in on their messages."

Her father gazed at the screen, analysing the Streams'

movements.

"You can do this Alandra, I believe in you. You've done this kind of configuration a thousand times in different ways and I can help now I'm here. Tell me what you already tried?" He added encouraging her.

Together they took over the controls of Zana and tapped into the core system. The tracker was blinking on and off in three sectors of the grid. The curser swung to the left one, zooming in on the movement and messages that were engaged in full flow. "Over there to the left," she said. Someone was messaging to their contact. "It's at the end of the rock face," a response came back. Alandra could sense it was the Streams camped outside of the Belnite plantation. They were looking for something that was moving close to their base.

"No, it's too close," said Alandra frustrated as she hooked into the next signal. The monitor circled, computed through several network nodes and then zoomed into a communication way out to the right of their position. There it was. She amplified the sound of them talking and simultaneously zoomed into the messages that were being exchanged with a position that appeared to be back in Reviathan. It was somewhere central, that's all that she could make out as the coordinates weren't explicit.

"Probably they haven't decided where to send the water, which flow to connect it to," she thought. "That's it, they must still be discussing the ideal place which is why they're stalling. We have a little more time," she thought.

"Still awaiting confirmation," she heard one of them say. The Stream next to him was communicating through his

MessagePad to Dorzak himself. "Everything is set," she heard him say. "Where are we sending it?" He asked.

"Now," said Alandra, "we have to upload the scrambler now. Sionis? Where are you?"

He blinked onto Zana's monitor at that moment.

"I'm here, where did you think I was?" He asked laughing. Just because I'm not standing there doesn't mean I can't hear every word you're saying," he grinned widely. "I could even change some of them if I want to," he added sarcastically.

"Not the time for practical jokes, " Alandra said curtly. "Can you scramble their communication? It's at coordinates…"

"I know where it is," said Sionis huffing indignantly. "I'm tracking you tracking them don't forget. I didn't miss anything."

"Well just get on with it then!" Alandra almost shouted and then restrained herself. *"Please!"*

"But where do I send it instead then, smart ?" He asked. "There is probably like 15 tonnes of water going to come flooding through there shortly. I can't just send it anywhere and in any case that would be a huge waste of resources. I'd rather the Streams had it than it was lost forever, splattered all over some desolate area of New Earth." Sionis concluded.

"Sionis, you're muttering," said Alandra "send it to the central Reviathan tank system."

"Can't do that," replied Gregoriat, "they'll think we stole it instead!"

"Good point," said Alandra wondering why she hadn't thought of that. "Well we'll just have to send it back down where it came from, in a loop. Can you scramble the coordinates to set a loop Sionis?"

"Sure, piece of cake," he replied confidently. "You're going to thank me for this for a very long time," He added still grinning widely as he enjoyed the limelight of attention being firmly fixed on his scrambling skills. It was so rare that Alandra needed to ask him for anything that he was literally revelling in the moment. Then he concentrated himself once again to infiltrate the system. Alandra's father Gregoriat was in the meantime checking the coordinates of the underground water source.

"It should be at 33°46'N, 120°39'E," he announced.

"Got it," replied Sionis. "Scrambling set and ready to roll. They should think that the message is coming from the main Stream encampment in Reviathan." He added as he set the system blinking. Zana was very excited indeed to be part of all these exchanges. This beat monitoring plants any day! So much so that she short-circuited for a nano-second. It was just enough to break the connection with the scrambler that in that instant turned into the next available network.

"Nooooo," Sionis yelled. "Not that way…."

The diverter zipped off onto the network below, looking in the wrong direction for the message to hook into. It scanned left and right but couldn't find its way back to the right path in the network and meanwhile the Streams' message with the coordinates was blipping happily towards its destination in Reviathan.

Alandra and Sionis looked at each other in disbelief. They'd missed their chance. Zana's screen was blinking calmly. A lone dot in the upper right-hand side of the screen where the scrambler had parked itself to wait for instructions. The communication network was all quiet across New Earth. In the silence, there was the painful realisation that the coordinates had been sent. It takes only a fraction of a second for the instructions to pass through. The Streams' plan was in operation.

"Follow the message trail!" Their father suggested. "At least we'll know where they're taking the supplies." He leapt towards Zana's controls and started to send instructions to work out where the Stream's message had landed.

"There it is," Sionis shouted, finding his enthusiasm again. "It's behind the fountains of Eastern sector 8. They're planning to store it in the underground tanks there."

"I wonder where they'll take it next?" Alandra asked out loud. "If you had that much extra water and wanted to make a profit, what would you do with it?"

"Sell it to the nomads of New Earth, the Stars!" Sionis deduced. "I heard that water was becoming so rare that they're willing to pay a high price for making sure that they can continue to live as they choose, keeping their freedom and their ability to mediate wherever it's needed."

"Their horses need water too," added Alandra. "I heard that many of them had died from drinking from the toxic rivers in desperation."

"So how would they get it to them?" Asked Sionis.

"Of course! The merchants in Sector Four, the Spark tribe recluses," replied Alandra. "They're going to make it look like the Sparks cleaned the water themselves in order for it to be fit to sell. Many of the nomads pass through that way to cross over into New Earth along with other adventurers seeking new minerals. It would be the perfect market for reselling without anyone suspecting. All they'd need to do is pay a small commission to the merchants."

"But that's peanuts," said Gregoriat "in comparison with what they could do with a large quantity of water. I'm not sure Dorzak would waste his time on such a small operation. My logic is telling me that he's planning to store a good amount of it for later, when there isn't enough water left on Reviathan, or even sell it back to the New Earthers in exchange for other resources!"

"They must be planning to extract at least 30 litres per second. That's enormous!," Sionis calculated. "You can't put that quantity just anywhere without being noticed."

"The fountain's storage space is too small in Sector 8," Alandra said shaking her head.

"Your mother mentioned something about her radars capturing movements in the Northern plains around two weeks ago. Some kind of construction. Do you think it could be that they are building a dedicated storage area far from the encampments?" Their father asked out loud.

"If that's where it's eventually going then we can head them off. We need a plan," Alandra concluded. "We'll need to be quick but organised."

"Now that they have sent the coordinates, I guess we have around two hours before they start to actually channel the water resources over there. They'll have to be careful not to be seen of course. There is a high probability that they'll wait for nightfall."

The three sat down to plan their counter-attack.

"We won't let you down Grandma," Alandra heard herself whisper in her mind. She felt a sudden warm sensation, almost as if someone had wrapped a warm blanket around her.

At that moment Sketch came back into the room. "Ready to go!" He beamed. "Eight of us will go back to the village to warn them. Four Seasons and four New Earthers. What's the plan?"

"We're just putting one together," replied Alandra. "We think we know where the water will be taken."

"So I'm just in time!" Smiled Sketch.

Everyone spoke animatedly and had thoughts about how it might work out. Each person's role was agreed and all the steps, including a back-up plan were drawn up.

"That should work," Alandra beamed although still feeling quite anxious. She scanned everyone's thoughts quickly to make sure there were no last hesitations. It was calm, there was nothing more to say.

Everyone took a deep breath. "Ok, let's get to it. No time to lose," Gregoriat added. "Good luck to you all, just do your best."

They nodded and parted directions. Gregoriat and Sionis stayed at Zana's control panel while Alandra prepared herself to leave with Sketch's party. She wrapped the book carefully into her pack and covered herself with her cloak.

"Remember, the radars won't protect you once you pass through the perimeter fence. It's only eighty meters. The Seasons will need to be ready." Gregoriat called after his daughter as she disappeared towards the tunnel hatch.

At the entrance, the party were assembled and awaiting instructions. Alandra and Sketch looked at one another for reassurance. Sketch nodded. "Let's do it!" He said confidently to everyone. "The villagers need to know. We only have one hour to get there."

The Seasons gathered around Alandra as they left the protection of Belnite's underground tunnels. The Streams noticing their movement, intensified their assault. They called the wind from all directions, linking arms to group their channeling abilities. The force was intense but the Seasons stood fast, huddled around Alandra. Against the storm that was raging around them once again, Sketch's party urged forward. The Seasons had such determination in their hearts that it would take a mountain to stop them. They had no choice but to arrive at the village, the future of Belnite and many other parts of New Earth depended on it. They couldn't let them steal Earth's precious water resources. They also now knew that extra water resources existed that could save other part of the Earth.

With every step their courage became stronger but the intensity of the wind was also increasing so they had to walk slowly.

"At this speed it might take them more than the two hours to get there, by then the water might be gone forever," thought Sketch.

He had been analysing the cliffs for weeks now and knew them off by heart. He swiftly left the party and forced his way round to the side of the rock face where once again it was protected from the wind that was raging around him. He began to scale the side, placing his hands and feet carefully and skilfully in the small cracks to edge himself higher. As he did so, he started to imagine all of the different scenarios of how he might be able to stop the Streams. Distract them? Separate them? Could he even capture them in some way? All he needed was to stall them for a few minutes in order for Alandra and the rest of the party to make enough progress out of the area of the storm. Then a thought came to him.

He came to a pause behind a group of rocks to the rear of where the Stream tribespeople were standing on the edge of the cliff. He started to make scratching noises and little by little imitate the scuffles and movements of a wild animal. Then growling as if preparing an attack. One of the Streams noticed the sound and turned their head. She nudged the Stream next to her to listen.

"There, behind those rocks,' she said. The other Stream encouraged her to continue concentrating but her attention was already elsewhere. She was too scared that there might be a wolf. Sketch increased the sound and it worked, she broke off from the group for a moment to move to a safer spot. The others also noticed the noise and one decided to investigate, by which stage Sketch was already on his way back down again to join the party heading towards the village. They had picked up speed and were marching joyfully in the hope of arriving quickly now the storm had died down.

Over at the New Earther's encampment, the villagers were preparing to receive the water supplies. Tanks and irrigation systems were being put into place and the area was alight with celebration. People were dancing and singing. Children were running around excitedly and getting under the feet of the workers. Everyone was imagining what their new life would be like without having to walk so far for their resources.

Many of the elders were gathering the remaining seeds that they had to plant. No-one planted anymore because of the harsh conditions. These grains had been kept as family heirlooms for decades, hoping that they would eventually provide the community with food once again. There were grains for apple trees, potatoes, cassava, carrots, and peppers. The group were animatedly discussing where to plant each of them and the conditions that would be necessary for them to survive.

They were so busy that they did not notice that the Streams were about to divert some of the resources. They were blinded by the anticipation of a better life and all the pleasures that would come with it. A signal came through to the Streams at the surface. They entered the coordinates into their MessagePads once again, along with other details of volume and speed to calculate how long it would take for the water to arrive at its destination. A first proportion was set to be transferred to the central fountains of Reviathan. A chain of Streams had been strategically placed between the village and the cross-over to Reviathan to move the water kinetically, just like a relay race. From that point, the group had installed transparent pipelines out across the sea and back to Reviathan. These same pipes would also be used for the second transfer of resources but this time they would have to stretch to the Northern plains where it would be stored for some time.

One of the Streams nodded and the diversion began.

"Noooooo!" Cried Sionis who was watching the countdown from Zana's monitor.

12

Showdown

As the party entered the village, Sketch immediately lifted his arms in the air to alert everyone of their arrival. They hurried towards the chief who was sitting in the far corner of the main square. He was surrounded by six of the other elders and they were discussing the next stage of the plans. The encampment was alive with people bustling around making preparations for the new irrigation system, whilst they were determining whether a reorganisation of the village itself was necessary. There were tanks full of water that people were starting the draw from. It was clear as Sketch approached that they were in no mood to be disturbed.

Despite greeting them respectfully, he was brushed away and encouraged to come back later. One of the elders even waved his staff at them in frustration when Sketch refused to leave.

They looked up, one by one from their conversation. Then, noticing the presence of Alandra and the Seasons tribesmen, there was a moment of silence.

"What are they doing here?" The chief asked skeptically.

"They are here to help us," replied Sketch "we are being scammed," He added.

Dorzak had appeared at the far corner of the village square and as he caught sight of the party, he strode firmly towards them.

The chief laughed, "what do you mean young man? Can't you see that the village is about to live one of the most incredible transformations in it's history? Do you have no eyes?"

"We have to look further than our eyes allow us to see sometimes," Sketch replied.

"Such impertinence!" Replied another elder. "What would you know about what is right for our village?"

"Nothing, I guess," admitted Sketch, "but I know when I'm being misled."

Alandra stepped forward greeting the group reverently. She reached into her pack to reveal the book which she laid out on the ground in front of them. As she did so, the Seasons tribesmen made a circle around her as protection.

"This is the Book of Prophecies," she offered, "have you heard of it?"

The elders shook their heads. The markings on the cover glinted in the midday sun, making them squint. She opened it quickly to the page about their village.

"It has just come into our possession. It describes the three potential destinies of mankind," she continued. "One of them talks of your people, of the New Earthers being used to steal resources. We knew it was important to share this information with you. Look at this picture."

At this point Dorzak arrived at the group.

"What is the problem here? He asked. "We have so much to do to upgrade the village. Who are these people wasting our time?"

Alandra threw a cold glance at him. She could read in his thoughts that he was scanning through multiple possibilities to cover over whatever story they were here to share. The connections were fast and Alandra had difficulty concentrating on those while also keeping her attention on the rest of the group. His eyes sparkled. Somehow he didn't appear to be scared of them. She turned her attention back to the elders who were clearly now in confusion. Their thoughts were shifting to being defensive because some doubt had crept into their minds.

"You are the girl who translates for the Seasons aren't you?" One of the New Earthers asked aggressively. "What interest do you have with our business? Are you once again trying to tell us what to do? Can you not trust us to manage our own affairs? Are we not your elders? Surely we can see how to manage our infrastructure without the interference of a small girl like you!" He sneered.

Alandra was unphased. She looked directly at him and was suddenly filled with confidence in the fact that she was surrounded by her ancestors, remembering what they had said about her. How she told the truth and would say what others wouldn't. Instead of being annoyed by the elder's remark, she remembered the GRACE model that her mother had taught her as a child. The steps flashed through her mind. 1. Gather and concentrate your attention; 2. Remember your intention (what was motivating her to be there at this time); 3. Align yourself with the other person (notice your and their emotions and body language, leaving space for the interaction to flow); 4. Consider what might best serve the situation (how can I help? Think of all of your skills and experience but be open to new facts and learning so as not to draw hasty conclusions); 5. Engage in a fashion that develops mutual respect. She took a deep breath.

"I appreciate that I might be young and I do not have your experience, but I do have proof that your water is being stolen, right as we speak, and the more we speak, the less will remain. It is your water, not mine. I have no interest in it, except for in the future of New Earth. I have an interest in ensuring that neither New Earthers, nor Reviathaners perish. I made a promise to my ancestors to protect the contents of this book and I choose to use my integrity to do just that."

Dorzak was infuriated by the honesty of Alandra's statement. His eyes filled with malice.

"Who is this troublemaker that thinks she can just walk in here and ruin our plans. With a book from her ancestors, not ours and demand that we listen to her. Is she perhaps jealous of the progress you are making? Has she something to gain herself from these resources? Careful, you remember I warned you that Reviathan is seeking to extend into New Earth and take its resources for their growing populations. Did I not alert you to this danger?" He added calmly, suddenly feeling satisfied at finding an argument that would ignite the villagers' paranoia.

As he spoke, the party saw his fellow Streams tribespeople arriving in reinforcement behind him. Six, seven, eight of them. They had left their work diverting the water to come to his aid.

"Let us help you to rid yourselves of these troublemakers," Dorzak offered, raising his arms to call up the elements.

Sketch realised it was time to intervene. "No," he stated assertively, "I have seen the book. I know what it says. We will find ourselves in slavery if we choose to believe this man!"

"Lies!" Cried Dorzak in fury. "What is this ingratitude? I have shown you only kindness in helping you to access the resources you need."

"I will show you," Alandra offered as she turned another page of the book and advanced slightly to show them.

In a flash Dorzak whipped up a burst of wind to sweep the book away from her. The Seasons, seeing his attempt, formed a stronger circle around her, planting their feet into the ground and calling for strength from the Earth to protect her. The pages flipped over but Alandra held on tight. She knew she had to show them the scenes of their village. They would see how Dorzak was manipulating them. She could read the confusion in their thoughts. Against the wind that was raging, she opened the book to the right page and raised it high in front of her for them all to see. As she did so she spoke aloud the text beside it. It was as if it came to her automatically, she didn't need to read it. She was once again surrounded by her ancestors, who formed a semi-circle in front of her. Her courage grew from seeing them once again. Her red locks flapped wildly in the wind and her eyes grew bright and determined. The louder she spoke, the more Dorzak attempted to raise the force of the wind around her. The villagers could barely hear, despite her valiant efforts.

Several of the Streams noticed that there were fires lit in random areas around the village. The Streams raised their hands, calling the fire element towards them, which they shaped into tiny balls of fire that they proceeded to launch at the party to scare them. The villagers stood with their mouths aghast as they witnessed the battle that was taking form around them. Many of them ran for cover but the elders remained, unphased but wondering what was going on.

"Now you will stop!" Dorzak called to them.

The firebombs continued to distract the villagers. The Seasons skin thickened like armadillos as they formed a dome around her. Their determination was strong, but in a sudden burst of lightening sent by Dorzak, the book was thrown 10 meters away from the party. Alandra was shocked but kept speaking the text as if she was still in a trance. The villagers stared at her, mesmerised by what was happening.

One of the Streams picked up the book and tucked it under his arm. Sketch dived towards him having witnessed the scene from beside Alandra, but it was too late. The Stream created a burst of tornado under his feet to propel him to the safety of some nearby rocks. Sketch dodged the firebombs here and there as he sprinted after the Stream. It was too much for him to imagine that the book could get away. What a catastrophe if it was to fall into the hands of Dorzak!

Sketch scaled the rocks to catch up to the Stream tribesman who was watching the battle below and determining his options for escaping to safety. He signalled to another Stream to his left who started running towards him to help. The Stream propelled a bolt of lightening towards Sketch to push him off balance but Sketch was a skilled climber. He managed at the last moment to swing to one side of the burst and stretched upwards to cling to a rock that pulled him closer to his adversary. He jumped from rock to rock, scaling higher and closer to him but just as he was arriving at the top, the Stream threw the book into the air away from him. Sketch's heart sank as he watched it launch away from him, almost in slow motion. Both Streams sent a tornado of wind towards it to catch and then hold it steady in the air. It was far too high for Sketch to reach and he had to watch reluctantly as both Streams followed after it, propelled by their own tornados.

Dorzak smiled widely seeing his fellow Steams disappearing into the distance with the book. It was now in their possession. He turned his attention back to Alandra who was still somehow reciting the text. He concentrated to call up a ball of lightening that he intended to shock the Seasons into dispersing around her.

Then suddenly the whole area around the Seasons was covered by a protective shield. It circulated around them in pale blue light rings, giving out a slight humming noise.

Sionis flipped onto Alandra's MessagePad screen surprising her out of her trance. "Yahoo!" He yelled, "it worked! Mum changed the coordinates of the radars away from the plantation. We have your coordinates at the village. You only have a surface area of 80 metres each side, don't venture outside and you'll be safe."

Dorzak lowered his hands and let the lightening dispel as he realised that the party were now inaccessible. The elders looked at him questioningly. They had heard much of what Alandra had been sharing and his attacks on the Seasons seemed excessive for someone who had nothing to hide. They stood in front of him defiantly, asking for explanations of what he was really intending.

His eyes flickered with malice. He laughed and then in an instant, he also created a tornado of wind which lifted him to safety above the group. His followers also ceased their fire attacks and joined him, gathering around. It was an awry sight. Six Streams all looking down on the villagers and Seasons below. They appeared surreal to the villagers. These were powers that they had never encountered and they realised that they had been mesmerised by them. So much so it had blinded them to the truth that they were being manipulated. In an instant, the group of Streams turned and made their escape. Their plans had been exposed and there was nothing left to do here. They had already started to divert a certain volume of water so made off with what they had managed to take already and after all they now had the most important element, the Book of Prophesies.

Watching them move into the distance everyone felt relieved, but the book was now outside of the protective care of Reviathan and they couldn't let it remain in Dorzak's hands.

Alandra was filled with panic as she realised that it was gone. Her heart felt heavy and tears filled her eyes as she thought about the fact that she had let her ancestors down. She forced the tears back, not letting herself cry, she instead became angry. How could this have happened? This wasn't how it was supposed to happen!

"This is not the end," she heard her Grandmother whisper to her. "It is just the start. It marks a new beginning for the villagers, one of freedom and progression. There are now only two future possibilities."

"But the book?" Sighed Alandra. "How can we confront them without the Book of Prophecies?"

"You will see my dear," replied her Grandmother, "nothing is ever lost, there is possibility in every moment. It is for you to use your courage to seize the opportunities that will present themselves to you."

Alandra nodded and her anger subsided. The important thing right now was to ensure that the resources were protected. The villagers rushed to the entrance of the caves. Now that they were no longer blinded by the idea of everything being perfect, they could see the deception that Dorzak had started to put in place. They saw for themselves the pipes leading out towards the sea where the water was to be smuggled out. As they checked the levels of the water reserves, they could see that already, many gallons had been stolen and they looked at one another for reassurance that it would all be ok.

The chief came to the front to inspect the extent of the losses. He bowed his head in sadness. "I was blinded by what I thought was progress," he admitted. He carefully removed his cloak and his staff and placed them down as an offering in front of the resources. "I have let you down. It is time for me to take my leave. Someone else will lead you now," he added and he turned to walk back to his quarters solemnly.

Sketch and Alandra exchanged glances. They knew that the book was gone but that they had headed off the second possibility. The villagers were now free to choose their destiny and that was a moment to celebrate.